HERE AND BEYOND

BY

EDITH WHARTON

British Library Cataloguing-in-Publication Data
A catalogue record for this book is available from the
British Library

CONTENTS

CONTENTS

CONTENTS

Edith Wharton

Edith Wharton was born in New York City in 1862. Her family were extremely wealthy, and during her youth she was provided private tuition and travelled extensively in Europe. A voracious reader, Wharton studied literature, philosophy, science, and art, and began to write poetry and short fiction. In 1885, aged 23, Edith married a banker, Edward Robbins, and for the next few years they travelled extensively together. Living near Central Park in New York, Wharton's first poems were published in *Scribner's Magazine*. In 1891, the same publication printed the first of her many short stories, titled 'Mrs. Manstey's View'. Over the next four decades, they – along with other well-established American publications such as *Atlantic Monthly*, *Century Magazine*, *Harper's* and *Lippincott's* – regularly published her work.

A lifelong keen architect, in 1902 Wharton designed and built her home, The Mount, in Lenox, Massachusetts. It was while living here that she wrote many of her works, including the 1905 novel *The House of Mirth*, which was that year's bestseller, and is now considered a classic of American literary Naturalism. In the period leading up to the First World War, Wharton wrote prolifically, and in 1921 she received the Pulitzer Prize – the first ever woman to do so – for her novel *The Age of Innocence*. Like much of her work, the novel examines the tension between societal pressures and the pursuit of genuine happiness, and includes careful use of dramatic irony.

Edith Wharton died of a stroke in 1937, aged 75. In addition to her novels, she is remembered for her short fiction, especially her excellent ghost stories.

MISS MARY PASK

CHAPTER I

It was not till the following spring that I plucked up courage to tell Mrs. Bridgeworth what had happened to me that night at Morgat.

In the first place, Mrs. Bridgeworth was in America; and after the night in question I lingered on abroad for several months--not for pleasure, God knows, but because of a nervous collapse supposed to be the result of having taken up my work again too soon after my touch of fever in Egypt. But, in any case, if I had been door to door with Grace Bridgeworth I could not have spoken of the affair before, to her or to any one else; not till I had been rest-cured and built up again at one of those wonderful Swiss sanatoria where they clean the cobwebs out of you. I could not even have written to her--not to save my life. The happenings of that night had to be overlaid with layer upon layer of time and forgetfulness before I could tolerate any return to them.

The beginning was idiotically simple; just the sudden reflex of a New England conscience acting on an enfeebled constitution. I had been painting in Brittany, in lovely but uncertain autumn weather, one day all blue and silver, the next shrieking gales or driving fog. There is a rough little white-washed inn out on the Pointe du Raz, swarmed over

9

by tourists in summer but a sea-washed solitude in autumn; and there I was staying and trying to do waves, when some one said: "You ought to go over to Cape something else, beyond Morgat."

I went, and had a silver-and-blue day there; and on the way back the name of Morgat set up an unexpected association of ideas: Morgat--Grace Bridgeworth--Grace's sister, Mary Pask--"You know my darling Mary has a little place now near Morgat; if you ever go to Brittany do go to see her. She lives such a lonely life--it makes me so unhappy."

That was the way it came about. I had known Mrs. Bridgeworth well for years, but had only a hazy intermittent acquaintance with Mary Pask, her older and unmarried sister. Grace and she were greatly attached to each other, I knew; it had been Grace's chief sorrow, when she married my old friend Horace Bridgeworth, and went to live in New York, that Mary, from whom she had never before been separated, obstinately lingered on in Europe, where the two sisters had been travelling since their mother's death. I never quite understood why Mary Pask refused to join Grace in America. Grace said it was because she was "too artistic"--but, knowing the elder Miss Pask, and the extremely elementary nature of her interest in art, I wondered whether it were not rather because she disliked Horace Bridgeworth. There was a third alternative--more conceivable if one knew Horace-- and that was that she may have liked him too much. But that again became untenable (at least I supposed it did) when one knew Miss Pask: Miss Pask with her round flushed face, her innocent bulging eyes, her old-maidish flat decorated with art-tidies, and her vague and timid philanthropy. Aspire to Horace--!

Well, it was all rather puzzling, or would have been if it had been interesting enough to be worth puzzling over. But it was not. Mary Pask was like hundreds of other dowdy old maids, cheerful derelicts content with their innumerable little substitutes for living. Even Grace would not have interested me particularly if she hadn't happened to marry one of my oldest friends, and to be kind to his friends. She was a handsome capable and rather dull woman, absorbed in her husband and children, and without an ounce of imagination; and between her attachment to her sister and Mary Pask's worship of her there lay the inevitable gulf between the feelings of the sentimentally unemployed and those whose affections are satisfied. But a close intimacy had linked the two sisters before Grace's marriage, and Grace was one of the sweet conscientious women who go on using the language of devotion about people whom they live happily without seeing; so that when she said: "You know it's years since Mary and I have been together--not since little Molly was born. If only she'd come to America! Just think...Molly is six, and has never seen her darling auntie..." when she said this, and added: "If you go to Brittany promise me you'll look up my Mary," I was moved in that dim depth of one where unnecessary obligations are contracted.

And so it came about that, on that silver-and-blue afternoon, the idea "Morgat--Mary Pask--to please Grace" suddenly unlocked the sense of duty in me. Very well: I would chuck a few things into my bag, do my day's painting, go to see Miss Pask when the light faded, and spend the night at the inn at Morgat. To this end I ordered a rickety one-horse vehicle to await me at the inn when I got back from my painting, and in it I started out toward sunset to hunt for Mary Pask...

As suddenly as a pair of hands clapped over one's eyes, the sea-fog shut down on us. A minute before we had been driving over a wide bare upland, our backs turned to a sunset that crimsoned the road ahead; now the densest night enveloped us. No one had been able to tell me exactly where Miss Pask lived; but I thought it likely that I should find out at the fishers' hamlet toward which we were trying to make our way. And I was right...an old man in a doorway said: Yes--over the next rise, and then down a lane to the left that led to the sea; the American lady who always used to dress in white. Oh, *he* knew...near the *Baie des Trépassés*.

"Yes; but how can we see to find it? I don't know the place," grumbled the reluctant boy who was driving me.

"You will when we get there," I remarked.

"Yes--and the horse foundered meantime! I can't risk it,

sir; I'll get into trouble with the *patron*."

Finally an opportune argument induced him to get out and lead the stumbling horse, and we continued on our way. We seemed to crawl on for a long time through a wet blackness impenetrable to the glimmer of our only lamp. But now and then the ball lifted or its folds divided; and then our feeble light would drag out of the night some perfectly commonplace object--a white gate, a cow's staring face, a heap of roadside stones--made portentous and incredible by being thus detached from its setting, capriciously thrust at us, and as suddenly withdrawn. After each of these projections the darkness grew three times as thick; and the sense I had had for some time of descending a gradual slope now became that of scrambling down a precipice. I jumped out hurriedly and joined my young driver at the horse's head.

"I can't go on--I won't, sir!" he whimpered.

"Why, see, there's a light over there--just ahead!"

The veil swayed aside, and we beheld two faintly illuminated squares in a low mass that was surely the front of a house.

"Get me as far as that--then you can go back if you like."

The veil dropped again; but the boy had seen the lights and took heart. Certainly there was a house ahead of us; and certainly it must be Miss Pask's, since there could hardly be two in such a desert. Besides, the old man in the hamlet had said: "Near the sea"; and those endless modulations of the ocean's voice, so familiar in every corner of the Breton land that one gets to measure distances by them rather than by visual means, had told me for some time past that we must be making for the shore. The boy continued to lead the horse on without making any answer. The fog had shut in more closely than ever, and our lamp merely showed us the big round drops of wet on the horse's shaggy quarters.

The boy stopped with a jerk. "There's no house--we're going straight down to the sea."

"But you saw those lights, didn't you?"

"I thought I did. But where are they now? The fog's thinner again. Look--I can make out trees ahead. But there are no lights any more."

"Perhaps the people have gone to bed," I suggested jocosely.

"Then hadn't we better turn back, sir?"

"What--two yards from the gate?"

The boy was silent: certainly there was a gate ahead, and presumably, behind the dripping trees, some sort of dwelling. Unless there was just a field and the sea...the sea whose hungry voice I heard asking and asking, close below us. No wonder the place was called the Bay of the Dead! But what could have induced the rosy benevolent Mary Pask to come and bury herself there? Of course the boy wouldn't wait for me...I knew that...the *Baie des Trépassés* indeed! The sea whined down there as if it were feeding-time, and the Furies, its keepers, had forgotten it...

There *was* the gate! My hand had struck against it. I felt along to the latch, undid it, and brushed between wet bushes to the house-front. Not a candle-glint anywhere. If the house were indeed Miss Pask's, she certainly kept early hours...

CHAPTER II

Night and fog were now one, and the darkness as thick as a blanket. I felt vainly about for a bell. At last my hand came in contact with a knocker and I lifted it. The clatter with which it fell sent a prolonged echo through the silence; but for a minute or two nothing else happened.

"There's no one there, I tell you!" the boy called impatiently from the gate.

But there was. I had heard no steps inside, but presently a bolt shot back, and an old woman in a peasant's cap pushed her head out. She had set her candle down on a table behind her, so that her face, aureoled with lacy wings, was in obscurity; but I knew she was old by the stoop of her shoulders and her fumbling movements. The candle-light, which made her invisible, fell full on my face, and she looked at me.

"This is Miss Mary Pask's house?"

"Yes, sir." Her voice--a very old voice--was pleasant enough, unsurprised and even friendly.

"I'll tell her," she added, shuffling off. "Do you think she'll see me?" I threw after her.

"Oh, why not? The idea!" she almost chuckled. As she retreated I saw that she was wrapped in a shawl and had a cotton umbrella under her arm. Obviously she was going out--perhaps going home for the night. I wondered if Mary

16

Pask lived all alone in her hermitage.

The old woman disappeared with the candle and I was left in total darkness. After an interval I heard a door shut at the back of the house and then a slow clumping of aged *sabots* along the flags outside. The old woman had evidently picked up her *sabots* in the kitchen and left the house. I wondered if she had told Miss Pask of my presence before going, or whether she had just left me there, the butt of some grim practical joke of her own. Certainly there was no sound within doors. The footsteps died out, I heard a gate click--then complete silence closed in again like the fog.

"I wonder--" I began within myself; and at that moment a smothered memory struggled abruptly to the surface of my languid mind.

"But she's *dead*--Mary Pask is *dead*!"

I almost screamed it aloud in my amazement. It was incredible, the tricks my memory had played on me since my fever! I had known for nearly a year that Mary Pask was dead--had died suddenly the previous autumn--and though I had been thinking of her almost continuously for the last two or three days it was only now that the forgotten fact of her death suddenly burst up again to consciousness.

Dead! But hadn't I found Grace Bridge-worth in tears and crape the very day I had gone to bid her good-bye before sailing for Egypt? Hadn't she laid the cable before my eyes, her own streaming with tears while I read: "Sister died suddenly this morning requested burial in garden of house particulars by letter"--with the signature of the American Consul at Brest, a friend of Bridgeworth's I seemed to recall? I could see the very words of the message printed on the darkness before me.

As I stood there I was a good deal more disturbed by the discovery of the gap in my memory than by the fact of being alone in a pitch-dark house, either empty or else inhabited by strangers. Once before of late I had noted this queer temporary blotting-out of some well-known fact; and here was a second instance of it. Decidedly, I wasn't as well over my illness as the doctors had told me...Well, I would get back to Morgat and lie up there for a day or two, doing nothing, just eating and sleeping...

In my self-absorption I had lost my bearings, and no longer remembered where the door was. I felt in every pocket in turn for a match--but since the doctors had made me give up smoking, why should I have found one?

The failure to find a match increased my sense of irritated helplessness, and I was groping clumsily about the hall among the angles of unseen furniture when a light slanted along the rough-cast wall of the stairs. I followed its direction, and on the landing above me I saw a figure in white shading a candle with one hand and looking down. A chill ran along my spine, for the figure bore a strange resemblance to that of Mary Pask as I used to know her.

"Oh, it's *you*!" she exclaimed in the cracked twittering voice which was at one moment like an old woman's quaver, at another like a boy's falsetto. She came shuffling down in her baggy white garments, with her usual clumsy swaying movements; but I noticed that her steps on the wooden stairs were soundless. Well--they would be, naturally!

I stood without a word, gazing up at the strange vision above me, and saying to myself: "There's nothing there, nothing whatever. It's your digestion, or your eyes, or some damned thing wrong with you somewhere--"

But there was the candle, at any rate; and as it drew nearer, and lit up the place about me, I turned and caught hold of the door-latch. For, remember, I had seen the cable, and Grace in crape...

"Why, what's the matter? I assure you, you don't disturb me!" the white figure twittered; adding, with a faint laugh: "I don't have so many visitors nowadays--"

She had reached the hall, and stood before me, lifting her candle shakily and peering up into my face. "You haven't changed--not as much as I should have thought. But I have, haven't I?" she appealed to me with another laugh; and abruptly she laid her hand on my arm. I looked down at the hand, and thought to myself: "*That* can't deceive me."

I have always been a noticer of hands. The key to character that other people seek in the eyes, the mouth, the modelling of the skull, I find in the curve of the nails, the cut of the finger-tips, the way the palm, rosy or sallow, smooth or seamed, swells up from its base. I remembered Mary Pask's hand vividly because it was so like a caricature of herself; round, puffy, pink, yet prematurely old and useless. And there, unmistakably, it lay on my sleeve: but changed and shrivelled--somehow like one of those pale freckled toadstools that the least touch resolves to dust...Well--to dust? Of course...

I looked at the soft wrinkled fingers, with their foolish little oval finger-tips that used to be so innocently and naturally pink, and now were blue under the yellowing nails--and my flesh rose in ridges of fear.

"Come in, come in," she fluted, cocking her white untidy head on one side and rolling her bulging blue eyes at me. The horrible thing was that she still practised the same arts, all the childish wiles of a clumsy capering coquetry. I felt her pull on my sleeve and it drew me in her wake like a steel cable.

The room she led me into was--well, "unchanged" is the term generally used in such cases. For as a rule, after people die, things are tidied up, furniture is sold, remembrances are despatched to the family. But some morbid piety (or Grace's instructions, perhaps) had kept this room looking exactly as I supposed it had in Miss Pask's lifetime. I wasn't in the mood for noting details; but in the faint dabble of moving candle-light I was half aware of bedraggled cushions, odds and ends of copper pots, and a jar holding a faded branch of some late-flowering shrub. A real Mary Pask "interior"!

The white figure flitted spectrally to the chimney-piece, lit two more candles, and set down the third on a table. I hadn't supposed I was superstitious--but those three candles! Hardly knowing what I did, I hurriedly bent and blew one out. Her laugh sounded behind me.

"Three candles--you still mind that sort of thing? I've got beyond all that, you know," she chuckled. "Such a comfort... such a sense of freedom..." A fresh shiver joined the others already coursing over me.

"Come and sit down by me," she entreated, sinking to a sofa. "It's such an age since I've seen a living being!"

Her choice of terms was certainly strange, and as she leaned back on the white slippery sofa and beckoned me with one of those unburied hands my impulse was to turn and run. But her old face, hovering there in the candle-light, with the unnaturally red cheeks like varnished apples and the blue eyes swimming in vague kindliness, seemed to appeal to me against my cowardice, to remind me that, dead or alive, Mary Pask would never harm a fly.

"Do sit down!" she repeated, and I took the other corner of the sofa.

"It's so wonderfully good of you--I suppose Grace asked you to come?" She laughed again--her conversation had always been punctuated by rambling laughter. "It's an event-

-quite an event! I've had so few visitors since my death, you see."

Another bucketful of cold water ran over me; but I looked at her resolutely, and again the innocence of her face disarmed me.

I cleared my throat and spoke--with a huge panting effort, as if I had been heaving up a grave-stone. "You live here alone?" I brought out.

"Ah, I'm glad to hear your voice--I still remember voices, though I hear so few," she murmured dreamily. "Yes--I live here alone. The old woman you saw goes away at night. She won't stay after dark...she says she can't. Isn't it funny? But it doesn't matter; I like the darkness." She leaned to me with one of her irrelevant smiles. "The dead," she said, "naturally get used to it."

Once more I cleared my throat; but nothing followed.

She continued to gaze at me with confidential blinks. "And Grace? Tell me all about my darling. I wish I could have seen her again...just once." Her laugh came out grotesquely. "When she got the news of my death--were you with her? Was she terribly upset?"

I stumbled to my feet with a meaningless stammer. I couldn't answer--I couldn't go on looking at her.

"Ah, I see...it's too painful," she acquiesced, her eyes brimming, and she turned her shaking head away.

"But after all...I'm glad she was so sorry...It's what I've been

longing to be told, and hardly hoped for. Grace forgets..."
She stood up too and flitted across the room, wavering
nearer and nearer to the door.

"Thank God," I thought, "she's going."

"Do you know this place by daylight?" she asked
abruptly.

I shook my head.

"It's very beautiful. But you wouldn't have seen *me* then.
You'd have had to take your choice between me and the
landscape. I hate the light--it makes my head ache. And
so I sleep all day. I was just waking up when you came."
She smiled at me with an increasing air of confidence. "Do
you know where I usually sleep? Down below there--in
the garden!" Her laugh shrilled out again. "There's a shady
corner down at the bottom where the sun never bothers one.
Sometimes I sleep there till the stars come out."

The phrase about the garden, in the consul's cable, came
back to me and I thought: "After all, it's not such an unhappy
state. I wonder if she isn't better off than when she was
alive?"

Perhaps she was--but I was sure I wasn't, in her company.
And her way of sidling nearer to the door made me distinctly
want to reach it before she did. In a rush of cowardice I
strode ahead of her--but a second later she had the latch in
her hand and was leaning against the panels, her long white
raiment hanging about her like grave-clothes. She drooped

her head a little sideways and peered at me under her lashless lids.

"You're not going?" she reproached me.

I dived down in vain for my missing voice, and silently signed that I was.

"Going going away? Altogether?" Her eyes were still fixed on me, and I saw two tears gather in their corners and run down over the red glistening circles on her cheeks. "Oh, but you mustn't," she said gently. "I'm too lonely..."

I stammered something inarticulate, my eyes on the blue-nailed hand that grasped the latch. Suddenly the window behind us crashed open, and a gust of wind, surging in out of the blackness, extinguished the candle on the nearest chimney-corner. I glanced back nervously to see if the other candle were going out too.

"You don't like the noise of the wind? I do. It's all I have to talk to...People don't like me much since I've been dead. Queer, isn't it? The peasants are so superstitious. At times I'm really lonely..." Her voice cracked in a last effort at laughter, and she swayed toward me, one hand still on the latch.

"Lonely, lonely! If you knew how *lonely*! It was a lie when I told you I wasn't! And now you come, and your face looks friendly...and you say you're going to leave me! No--no--no--you shan't! Or else, why did you come? It's cruel...I used to think I knew what loneliness was...after Grace married, you know. Grace thought she was always thinking of me, but she wasn't. She called me 'darling,' but she was thinking of her husband and children. I said to myself then: 'You couldn't be lonelier if you were dead.' But I know better now...There's been no loneliness like this last year's...none! And sometimes I sit here and think: 'If a man came along some day and took a fancy to you?'" She gave another wavering cackle. "Well, such things *have* happened, you know, even after youth's gone...a man who'd had his troubles too. But no one came till to-night...and now you say you're going!" Suddenly she flung herself toward me. "Oh, stay with me, stay with me...just tonight...It's so sweet and quiet here...No one need know...no one will ever come and trouble us."

I ought to have shut the window when the first gust came. I might have known there would soon be another, fiercer one. It came now, slamming back the loose-hinged lattice, filling the room with the noise of the sea and with wet swirls of fog, and dashing the other candle to the floor. The light went out, and I stood there--we stood there--lost to each other in the roaring coiling darkness. My heart seemed to stop beating; I had to fetch up my breath with great heaves that covered me with sweat. The door--the door--well, I knew I had been facing it when the candle went. Something white and wraithlike seemed to melt and crumple up before me in the night, and avoiding the spot where it had sunk away I stumbled around it in a wide circle, got the latch in my hand, caught my foot in a scarf or sleeve, trailing loose and invisible, and freed myself with a jerk from this last obstacle. I had the door open now. As I got into the hall I heard a whimper from the blackness behind me; but I scrambled on to the hall door, dragged it open and bolted out into the night. I slammed the door on that pitiful low whimper, and the fog and wind enveloped me in healing arms.

CHAPTER III

When I was well enough to trust myself to think about it all again I found that a very little thinking got my temperature up, and my heart hammering in my throat. No use...I simply couldn't stand it...for I'd seen Grace Bridgeworth in crape, weeping over the cable, and yet I'd sat and talked with her sister, on the same sofa--her sister who'd been dead a year!

The circle was a vicious one; I couldn't break through it. The fact that I was down with fever the next morning might have explained it; yet I couldn't get away from the clinging reality of the vision. Supposing it *was* a ghost I had been talking to, and not a mere projection of my fever? Supposing something survived of Mary Pask--enough to cry out to me the unuttered loneliness of a lifetime, to express at last what the living woman had always had to keep dumb and hidden? The thought moved me curiously--in my weakness I lay and wept over it. No end of women were like that, I supposed, and perhaps, after death, if they got their chance they tried to use it...Old tales and legends floated through my mind; the bride of Corinth, the mediaeval vampire--but what names to attach to the plaintive image of Mary Pask!

My weak mind wandered in and out among these visions and conjectures, and the longer I lived with them the more convinced I became that something *which had been Mary Pask* had talked with me that night...I made up my mind,

27

when I was up again, to drive back to the place (in broad daylight, this time), to hunt out the grave in the garden--that "shady corner where the sun never bothers one"--and appease the poor ghost with a few flowers. But the doctors decided otherwise; and perhaps my weak will unknowingly abetted them. At any rate, I yielded to their insistence that I should be driven straight from my hotel to the train for Paris, and thence transshipped, like a piece of luggage, to the Swiss sanatorium they had in view for me. Of course I meant to come back when I was patched up again...and meanwhile, more and more tenderly, but more intermittently, my thoughts went back from my snow-mountain to that wailing autumn night above the *Baie des Trépassés*, and the revelation of the dead Mary Pask who was so much more real to me than ever the living one had been.

CHAPTER IV

After all, why should I tell Grace Bridgeworth--ever? I had had a glimpse of things that were really no business of hers. If the revelation had been vouchsafed to me, ought I not to bury it in those deepest depths where the inexplicable and the unforgettable sleep together? And besides, what interest could there be to a woman like Grace in a tale she could neither understand nor believe in? She would just set me down as "queer"--and enough people had done that already. My first object, when I finally did get back to New York, was to convince everybody of my complete return to mental and physical soundness; and into this scheme of evidence my experience with Mary Pask did not seem to fit. All things considered, I would hold my tongue.

But after a while the thought of the grave began to trouble me. I wondered if Grace had ever had a proper grave-stone put on it. The queer neglected look of the house gave me the idea that perhaps she had done nothing--had brushed the whole matter aside, to be attended to when she next went abroad. "Grace forgets," I heard the poor ghost quaver...No, decidedly, there could be no harm in putting (tactfully) just that one question about the care of the grave; the more so as I was beginning to reproach myself for not having gone back to see with my own eyes how it was kept...

Grace and Horace welcomed me with all their old

friendliness, and I soon slipped into the habit of dropping in on them for a meal when I thought they were likely to be alone. Nevertheless my opportunity didn't come at once--I had to wait for some weeks. And then one evening, when Horace was dining out and I sat alone with Grace, my glance lit on a photograph of her sister--an old faded photograph which seemed to meet my eyes reproachfully.

"By the way, Grace," I began with a jerk, "I don't believe I ever told you: I went down to that little place of...of your sister's the day before I had that bad relapse."

At once her face lit up emotionally. "No, you never told me. How sweet of you to go!" The ready tears overbrimmed her eyes. "I'm so glad you did." She lowered her voice and added softly: "And did you see her?"

The question sent one of my old shudders over me. I looked with amazement at Mrs. Bridgeworth's plump face, smiling at me through a veil of painless tears. "I do reproach myself more and more about darling Mary," she added tremulously. "But tell me--tell me everything."

There was a knot in my throat; I felt almost as uncomfortable as I had in Mary Pask's own presence. Yet I had never before noticed anything uncanny about Grace Bridgeworth. I forced my voice up to my lips.

"Everything? Oh, I can't--." I tried to smile.

"But you did see her?"

I managed to nod, still smiling.

Her face grew suddenly haggard--yes, haggard! "And the change was so dreadful that you can't speak of it? Tell me--was that it?"

I shook my head. After all, what had shocked me was that the change was so slight--that between being dead and alive there seemed after all to be so little difference, except that of a mysterious increase in reality. But Grace's eyes were still searching me insistently. "You must tell me," she reiterated. "I know I ought to have gone there long ago--"

"Yes; perhaps you ought." I hesitated. "To see about the grave, at least..."

She sat silent, her eyes still on my face. Her tears had stopped, but her look of solicitude slowly grew into a stare of something like terror. Hesitatingly, almost reluctantly, she stretched out her hand and laid it on mine for an instant. "Dear old friend--" she began.

"Unfortunately," I interrupted, "I couldn't get back myself to see the grave...because I was taken ill the next day..."

"Yes, yes; of course. I know." She paused. "Are you *sure* you went there at all?" she asked abruptly.

"Sure? Good Lord--" It was my turn to stare. "Do you suspect me of not being quite right yet?" I suggested with an uneasy laugh.

"No--no...of course not...but I don't understand."

"Understand what? I went into the house...I saw everything, in fact, but her grave..."

"Her grave?" Grace jumped up, clasping her hands on her breast and darting away from me. At the other end of the room she stood and gazed, and then moved slowly back.

"Then, after all--I wonder?" She held her eyes on me, half fearful and half reassured. "Could it be simply that you never heard?"

"Never heard?"

"But it was in all the papers! Don't you ever read them? I meant to write...I thought I *had* written...but I said: 'At any rate he'll see it in the papers'...You know I'm always lazy about letters..."

"See what in the papers?"

"Why, that she *didn't* die...She isn't dead! There isn't any grave, my dear man! It was only a cataleptic trance...An extraordinary case, the doctors say...But didn't she tell you all about it--if you say you saw her?" She burst into half-hysterical laughter: "Surely she must have told you that she wasn't dead?"

"No," I said slowly, "she didn't tell me that."

We talked about it together for a long time after that--talked on till Horace came back from his men's dinner, after midnight. Grace insisted on going in and out of the whole subject, over and over again. As she kept repeating, it was certainly the only time that poor Mary had ever been in the papers. But though I sat and listened patiently I couldn't get up any real interest in what she said. I felt I should never again be interested in Mary Pask, or in anything concerning her.

THE YOUNG GENTLEMEN

CHAPTER I

The uniform newness of a new country gives peculiar relief to its few relics of antiquity--a term which, in America, may fairly enough be applied to any building already above ground when the colony became a republic.

Groups of such buildings, little settlements almost unmarred by later accretions, are still to be found here and there in the Eastern states; and they are always productive of inordinate pride in those who discover and live in them. A place of the sort, twenty years ago, was Harpledon, on the New England coast, somewhere between Salem and Newburyport. How intolerantly proud we all were of inhabiting it! How we resisted modern improvements, ridiculed fashionable "summer resorts," fought trolley-lines, overhead wires and telephones, wrote to the papers denouncing municipal vandalism, and bought up (those of us who could afford it) one little heavy-roofed house after another, as the land-speculator threatened them! All this, of course, was on a very small scale: Harpledon was, and is still, the smallest of towns, hardly more than a village, happily unmenaced by industry, and almost too remote for the week-end "flivver." And now that civic pride has taught Americans to preserve and adorn their modest monuments,

34

setting them in smooth stretches of turf and nursing the elms of the village green, the place has become far more attractive, and far worthier of its romantic reputation, than when we artists and writers first knew it. Nevertheless, I hope I shall never see it again; certainly I shall not if I can help it...

CHAPTER II

The elders of the tribe of summer visitors nearly all professed to have "discovered" Harpledon. The only one of the number who never, to my knowledge, put forth this claim was Waldo Cranch; and he had lived there longer than any of us.

The one person in the village who could remember his coming to Harpledon, and opening and repairing the old Cranch house (for his family had been India merchants when Harpledon was a thriving sea-port)--the only person who went back far enough to antedate Waldo Cranch was an aunt of mine, old Miss Lucilla Selwick, who lived in the Selwick house, itself a stout relic of India merchant days, and who had been sitting at the same window, watching the main street of Harpledon, for seventy years and more to my knowledge. But unfortunately the long range of Aunt Lucilla's memory often made it hit rather wide of the mark. She remembered heaps and heaps of far-off things; but she almost always remembered them wrongly. For instance, she used to say: "Poor Polly Everitt! How well I remember her, coming up from the beach one day screaming, and saying she'd seen her husband drowning before her eyes"--whereas every one knew that Mrs. Everitt was on a picnic when her husband was drowned at the other end of the world, and that no ghostly premonition of her loss had reached her. And whenever Aunt Lucilla mentioned Mr. Cranch's coming to live at Harpledon she used to say: "Dear me, I can see him now, driving by on that rainy afternoon in Denny Brine's old carry-all, with a great pile of bags and bundles, and on top of them a black and white hobby-horse with a real mane-- the very handsomest hobby-horse I ever saw." No persuasion could induce her to dissociate the image of this prodigious toy from her first sight of Waldo Cranch, most incurable of bachelors, and least concerned with the amusing of other people's children, even those of his best friends. In this case, to be sure, her power of evocation had a certain success. Some one told Cranch--Mrs. Durant I think it must have been--and I can still hear his hearty laugh.

"What could it have been that she saw?" Mrs. Durant questioned; and he responded gaily: "Why not simply the symbol of my numerous tastes?" Which--as Cranch painted and gardened and made music (even composed it)--seemed so happy an explanation that for long afterward the Cranch house was known to us as Hobby-Horse Hall.

It will be seen that Aunt Lucilla's reminiscences, though they sometimes provoked a passing amusement, were neither accurate nor illuminating. Naturally, nobody paid much attention to them, and we had to content ourselves with regarding Waldo Cranch, hale and hearty and social as he still was, as an Institution already venerable when the rest of us had first apprehended Harpledon. We knew, of course, the chief points in the family history: that the Cranches had been prosperous merchants for three centuries, and had intermarried with other prosperous families; that one of them, serving his business apprenticeship at Malaga in colonial days, had brought back a Spanish bride, to the bewilderment of Harpledon; and that Waldo Cranch himself had spent a studious and wandering youth in Europe. His Spanish great-grandmother's portrait still hung in the old house; and it was a long-standing joke at Harpledon that the young Cranch who went to Malaga, where he presumably had his pick of Spanish beauties, should have chosen so dour a specimen. The lady was a forbidding character on the canvas: very short and thickset, with a huge wig of black ringlets, a long harsh nose, and one shoulder perceptibly above the other. It was characteristic of Aunt Lucilla Selwick that in mentioning this swart virago she always took the tone of elegy. "Ah, poor thing, they say she never forgot the sunshine and orange blossoms, and pined off early, when her queer son Calvert was hardly out of petticoats. A strange man Calvert Cranch was; but he married Euphemia Waldo of Wood's Hole, the beauty, and had two sons, one exactly like Euphemia, the other made in his own image. And they do say that one was so afraid of his own face that he went back to Spain and died a monk--if you'll believe it," she always concluded with a Puritan shudder.

This was all we knew of Waldo Cranch's past; and he had

been so long a part of Harpledon that our curiosity seldom ranged beyond his coming there. He was our local ancestor; but it was a mark of his studied cordiality and his native tact that he never made us feel his priority. It was never he who embittered us with allusions to the picturesqueness of the old light-house before it was rebuilt, or the paintability of the vanished water-mill; he carried his distinction so far as to take Harpledon itself for granted, carelessly, almost condescendingly--as if there had been rows and rows of them strung along the Atlantic coast.

Yet the Cranch house was really something to brag about. Architects and photographers had come in pursuit of it long before the diffused quaintness of Harpledon made it the prey of the magazine illustrator. The Cranch house was not quaint; it owed little to the happy irregularities of later additions, and needed no such help. Foursquare and stern, built of a dark mountain granite (though all the other old houses in the place were of brick or wood), it stood at the far end of the green, where the elms were densest and the village street faded away between blueberry pastures and oakwoods.

A door with a white classical portico was the only eighteenth century addition. The house kept untouched its heavy slate roof, its low windows, its sober cornice and plain interior panelling--even the old box garden at the back, and the pagoda-roofed summer house, could not have been much later than the house. I have said that the latter owed little to later additions; yet some people thought the wing on the garden side was of more recent construction. If it was, its architect had respected the dimensions and detail of the original house, simply giving the wing one less story, and covering it with a lower-pitched roof. The learned thought that the kitchen and offices, and perhaps the slaves' quarters, had originally been in this wing; they based their argument on the fact of there being no windows, but only blind arches, on the side toward the garden, Waldo Cranch said he didn't know; he had found the wing just as it was now, with a big empty room on the ground floor, that he used for storing things, and a few low-studded bedchambers above. The house was so big that he didn't need any of these rooms, and had never bothered about them. Once, I remember, I thought him a little short with a fashionable Boston architect who had insisted on Mrs. Durant's bringing him to see the house, and who wanted to examine the windows on the farther, the invisible, side of the wing.

"Certainly," Cranch had agreed. "But you see those windows look on the kitchen-court and the drying-ground. My old housekeeper and the faithful retainers generally sit there in the afternoons in hot weather, when their work is done, and they've been with me so long that I respect their habits. At some other hour, if you'll come again--. You're going back to Boston tomorrow? So sorry! Yes, of course, you can photograph the front as much as you like. It's used to it." And he showed out Mrs. Durant and her protege.

When he came back a frown still lingered on his handsome brows. "I'm getting sick of having this poor old house lionized. No one bothered about it or me when I first came back to live here," he said. But a moment later he added, in his usual kindly tone: "After all, I suppose I ought to be pleased."

If anyone could have soothed his annoyance, and even made it appear unreasonable, it was Mrs. Durant. The fact that it was to her he had betrayed his impatience struck us all, and caused me to remark, for the first time, that she was the only person at Harpledon who was not afraid of him. Yes; we all were, though he came and went among us with such a show of good-fellowship that it took this trifling incident to remind me of his real aloofness. Not one of us but would have felt a slight chill at his tone to the Boston architect; but then I doubt if any of us but Mrs. Durant would have dared to bring a stranger to the house.

Mrs. Durant was a widow who combined gray hair with a still-youthful face at a time when this happy union was less generally fashionable than now. She had come to Harpledon among the earliest summer colonists, and had soon struck up a friendship with Waldo Cranch. At first Harpledon was sure they would marry; then it became sure they wouldn't; for a number of years now it had wondered why they hadn't.

These conjectures, of which the two themselves could hardly have been unaware, did not seem to trouble the even tenor of their friendship. They continued to meet as often as before, and Mrs. Durant continued to be the channel for transmitting any request or inquiry that the rest of us hesitated to put to Cranch. "We know he won't refuse you," I once said to her; and I recall the half-lift of her dark brows above a pinched little smile. "Perhaps," I thought, "he *has* refused her--once." If so, she had taken her failure gallantly, and Cranch appeared to find an undiminished pleasure in her company. Indeed, as the years went on their friendship grew closer; one would have said he was dependent on her if one could have pictured Cranch as dependent on anybody. But whenever I tried to do this I was driven back to the fundamental fact of his isolation.

"He could get on well enough without any of us," I thought to myself, wondering if this remoteness were inherited from the homesick Spanish ancestress. Yet I have seldom known a more superficially sociable man than Cranch. He had many talents, none of which perhaps went as far as he had once confidently hoped; but at least he used them as links with his kind instead of letting them seclude him in their jealous hold. He was always eager to show his sketches, to read aloud his occasional articles in the lesser literary reviews, and above all to play his new compositions to the musically-minded among us; or rather, since "eager" is hardly the term to apply to his calm balanced manner, I should say that he was affably ready to show off his accomplishments. But then he may have regarded doing so as one of the social obligations: I had felt from the first that, whatever Cranch did, he was always living up to some self-imposed and complicated standard. Even his way of taking off his hat struck me as the result of more thought than most people give to the act; his very absence of flourish lent it an odd importance.

CHAPTER III

It was the year of Harpledon's first "jumble sale" that all these odds and ends of observation first began to connect themselves in my mind.

Harpledon had decided that it ought to have a village hospital and dispensary, and Cranch was among the first to promise a subscription and to join the committee. A meeting was called at Mrs. Durant's and after much deliberation it was decided to hold a village fair and jumble sale in somebody's grounds; but whose? We all hoped Cranch would lend his garden; but no one dared to ask him. We sounded each other cautiously, before he arrived, and each tried to shift the enterprise to his neighbour; till at last Homer Davids, our chief celebrity as a painter, and one of the shrewdest heads in the community, said drily: "Oh, Cranch wouldn't care about it."

"How do you know he wouldn't?" some one queried.

"Just as you all do; if not, why is it that you all want some one else to ask him?"

Mrs. Durant hesitated. "I'm sure--" she began.

"Oh, well, all right, then! *You* ask him," rejoined Davids cheerfully.

"I can't always be the one--"

I saw her embarrassment, and volunteered: "If you think there's enough shade in my garden..."

By the way their faces lit up I saw the relief it was to them all not to have to tackle Cranch. Yet why, having a garden he was proud of, need he have been displeased at the request?

"Men don't like the bother," said one of our married ladies; which occasioned the proper outburst of praise for my unselfishness, and the observation that Cranch's maids, who had all been for years in his service, were probably set in their ways, and wouldn't care for the confusion and extra work. "Yes, old Catherine especially; she guards the place like a dragon," one of the ladies remarked; and at that moment Cranch appeared. Having been told what had been settled he joined with the others in complimenting me; and we began to plan for the jumble sale.

The men needed enlightenment on this point, I as much as the rest, but the prime mover immediately explained: "Oh, you just send any old rubbish you've got in the house."

We all welcomed this novel way of clearing out our cupboards, except Cranch who, after a moment, and with a whimsical wrinkling of his brows, said: "But I haven't got any old rubbish."

"Oh, well, children's cast-off toys for instance," a newcomer threw out at random.

There was a general smile, to which Cranch responded with one of his rare expressive gestures, as who should say: "*Toys*--in my house? But whose?"

I laughed, and one of the ladies, remembering our old

45

joke, cried out: "Why, but the hobby-horse!"

Cranch's face became a well-bred blank. Long-suffering courtesy was the note of the voice in which he echoed: "Hobbyhorse--?"

"Don't you remember?" It was Mrs. Durant who prompted him. "Our old joke? The wonderful black-and-white hobby-horse that Miss Lucilla Selwick said she saw you driving home with when you first arrived here? It had a real mane." Her colour rose a little as she spoke.

There was a moment's pause, while Cranch's brow remained puzzled; then a smile slowly cleared his face. "Of course!" he said. "I'd forgotten. Well, I feel now that I *was* young enough for toys thirty years ago; but I didn't feel so then. And we should have to apply to Miss Selwick to know what became of that hobby-horse. Meanwhile," he added, putting his hand in his pocket, "here's a small offering to supply some new ones for the fair."

The offering was not small: Cranch always gave liberally, yet always produced the impression of giving indifferently. Well, one couldn't have it both ways; some of our most gushing givers were the least lavish. The committee was delighted...

"It was queer," I said afterward to Mrs. Durant. "Why did the hobby-horse joke annoy Cranch? He used to like it."

She smiled. "He may think it's lasted long enough. Harpledon jokes *do* last, you know."

Yes; perhaps they did, though I had never thought of it

before.

"There's one thing that puzzles me," I went on; "I never know beforehand what is going to annoy him."

She pondered. "I'll tell you, then," she said suddenly. "It has annoyed him that no one thought of asking him to give one of his water-colours to the sale."

"Didn't we?"

"No. Homer Davids was asked, and that made it...rather more marked..."

"Oh, of course! I suppose we all forgot--"

She looked away. "Well," she said, "I don't suppose he likes to be forgotten."

"You mean: to have his accomplishments forgotten?"

"Isn't that a little condescending? I should say, his *gifts*," she corrected a trifle sharply. Sharpness was so unusual in her that she may have seen my surprise, for she added, in her usual tone: "After all, I suppose he's our most brilliant man, isn't he?" She smiled a little, as if to take the sting from my doing so.

"Of course he is," I rejoined. "But all the more reason-- how could a man of his kind resent such a trifling oversight? I'll write at once--"

"Oh, *don't!*" she cut me short, almost pleadingly.

Mrs. Durant's word was law: Cranch was not asked for a water-colour. Homer Davids's, I may add, sold for two thousand dollars, and paid for a heating-system for our hospital. A Boston millionaire came down on purpose to buy the picture. It was a great day for Harpledon.

CHAPTER IV

About a week after the fair I went one afternoon to call on Mrs. Durant, and found Cranch just leaving. His greeting, as he hurried by, was curt and almost hostile, and his handsome countenance so disturbed and pale that I hardly recognized him. I was sure there could be nothing personal in his manner; we had always been on good terms, and, next to Mrs. Durant, I suppose I was his nearest friend at Harpledon--if ever one could be said to get near Waldo Cranch! After he had passed me I stood hesitating at Mrs. Durant's open door--front doors at Harpledon were always open in those friendly days, except, by the way, Cranch's own, which the stern Catherine kept chained and bolted. Since meeting me could not have been the cause of his anger, it might have been excited by something which had passed between Mrs. Durant and himself; and if that were so, my call was probably inopportune. I decided not to go in, and was turning away when I heard hurried steps, and Mrs. Durant's voice. "Waldo!" she said.

I suppose I had always assumed that she called him so; yet the familiar appellation startled me, and made me feel more than ever in the way. None of us had ever given Cranch his Christian name.

Mrs. Durant checked her steps, perceiving that the back in the doorway was not Cranch's but mine. "Oh, do come in," she murmured, with an attempt at ease.

In the little drawing-room I turned and looked at her. She, too, was visibly disturbed; not angry, as he had been, but showing, on her white face and reddened lids, the pained reflection of his anger. Was it against her, then, that he had manifested it? Probably she guessed my thought, or felt her appearance needed to be explained, for she added quickly: "Mr. Cranch has just gone. Did he speak to you?"

"No. He seemed in a great hurry."

"Yes...I wanted to beg him to come back...to try to quiet him..."

She saw my bewilderment, and picked up a copy of an illustrated magazine which had been tossed on the sofa. "It's that--" she said.

The pages fell apart at an article entitled: "Colonial Harpledon," the greater part of which was taken up by a series of clever sketches signed by the Boston architect whom she had brought to Cranch's a few months earlier.

Of the six or seven drawings, four were devoted to the Cranch house. One represented the facade and its pillared gates, a second the garden front with the windowless side of the wing, the third a corner of the box garden surrounding the Chinese summer-house; while the fourth, a full-page drawing, was entitled: "The back of the slaves' quarters and service-court: quaint window-grouping."

On that picture the magazine had opened; it was evidently

the one which had been the subject of discussion between my hostess and her visitor.

"You see...you see..." she cried.

"This picture? Well, what of it? I suppose it's the far side of the wing--the side we've never any of us seen."

"Yes; that's just it. He's horribly upset..."

"Upset about what? I heard him tell the architect he could come back some other day and see the wing...some day when the maids were not sitting in the court; wasn't that it?"

She shook her head tragically. "He didn't mean it. Couldn't you tell by the sound of his voice that he didn't?"

Her tragedy airs were beginning to irritate me. "I don't know that I pay as much attention as all that to the sound of his voice."

She coloured, and choked back her tears. "I know him so well; I'm always sorry to see him lose his self-control. And then he considers me responsible."

"You?"

"It was I who took the wretched man there. And of course it was an indiscretion to do that drawing; he was never really authorized to come back. In fact, Mr. Cranch gave orders to Catherine and all the other servants not to let him in if he did."

"Well--?"

"One of the maids seems to have disobeyed the order; Mr. Cranch imagines she was bribed. He has been staying in Boston, and this morning, on the way back, he saw this magazine at the book-stall at the station. He was so horrified that he brought it to me. He came straight from the train without going home, so he doesn't yet know how the thing happened."

"It doesn't take much to horrify him," I said, again unable to restrain a faint sneer.

"What's the harm in the man's having made that sketch?"

"Harm?" She looked surprised at my lack of insight. "No actual harm, I suppose; but it was very impertinent; and Mr. Cranch resents such liberties intensely. He's so punctilious."

"Well, we Americans are not punctilious, and being one himself, he ought to know it by this time."

She pondered again. "It's his Spanish blood, I suppose... he's frightfully proud." As if this were a misfortune, she added: "I'm very sorry for him."

"So am I, if such trifles upset him."

Her brows lightened. "Ah, that's what I tell him--such things *are* trifles, aren't they? As I said just now: 'Your life's been too fortunate, too prosperous. That's why you're so easily put out.'"

"And what did he answer?"

"Oh, it only made him angrier. He said: 'I never expected that from *you*'--that was when he rushed out of the house." Her tears flowed over, and seeing her so genuinely perturbed I restrained my impatience, and took leave after a few words of sympathy.

Never had Harpledon seemed to me more like a tea-cup than with that silly tempest convulsing it. That there should be grownup men who could lose their self-command over such rubbish, and women to tremble and weep with them! For a moment I felt the instinctive irritation of normal man at such foolishness; yet before I reached my own door I was as mysteriously perturbed as Mrs. Durant.

The truth was, I had never thought of Cranch as likely to lose his balance over trifles. He had never struck me as unmanly; his quiet manner, his even temper, showed a sound sense of the relative importance of things. How then could so petty an annoyance have thrown him into such disorder?

I stopped short on my threshold, remembering his face as he brushed past me. "Something *is* wrong; really wrong," I thought. But what? Could it be jealousy of Mrs. Durant and the Boston architect? The idea would not bear a moment's consideration, for I remembered *her* face too.

"Oh, well, if it's his silly punctilio," I grumbled, trying to reassure myself, and remaining, after all, as much perplexed as before.

All the next day it poured, and I sat at home among my books. It must have been after ten in the evening when I was startled by a ring. The maids had gone to bed, and I went to the door, and opened it to Mrs. Durant. Surprised at the lateness of her visit, I drew her in out of the storm.

She had flung a cloak over her light dress, and the lace scarf on her head dripped with rain. Our houses were only a few hundred yards apart, and she had brought no umbrella, nor even exchanged her evening slippers for heavier shoes.

I took her wet cloak and scarf and led her into the library. She stood trembling and staring at me, her face like a marble mask in which the lips were too rigid for speech; then she laid a sheet of note-paper on the table between us. On it was written, in Waldo Cranch's beautiful hand: "My dear friend, I am going away on a journey. You will hear from me," with his initials beneath. Nothing more. The letter bore no date.

I looked at her, waiting for an explanation. None came. The first word she said was: "Will you come with me--now, at once?"

"Come with you--where?"

"To his house--before he leaves. I've only just got the letter, and I daren't go alone..."

"Go to Cranch's house? But I...at this hour...What is it you are afraid of?" I broke out, suddenly looking into her eyes.

She gave me back my look, and her rigid face melted. "I don't know--any more than you do--That's why I'm afraid."

"But I know nothing. What on earth has happened since I saw you yesterday?"

"Nothing till I got this letter."

"You haven't seen him?"

"Not since you saw him leave my house yesterday."

54

"Or had any message--any news of him?"

"Absolutely nothing. I've just sat and remembered his face."

My perplexity grew. "But surely you can't imagine...If you're as frightened as that you must have some other reason for it," I insisted.

She shook her head wearily. "It's the having none that frightens me. Oh, do come!"

"You think his leaving in this way means that he's in some kind of trouble?"

"In dreadful trouble."

"And you don't know why?"

"No more than you do!" she repeated.

I pondered, trying to avoid her entreating eyes. "But at this hour--come, do consider! I don't know Cranch so awfully well. How will he take it? You say he made a scene yesterday about that silly business of the architect's going to his house without leave..."

"That's just it. I feel as if his going away might be connected with that."

"But then he's mad!" I exclaimed. "No; not mad. Only--desperate."

I stood irresolute. It was evident that I had to do with a woman whose nerves were in fiddle-strings. What had reduced them to that state I could not conjecture, unless, indeed, she were keeping back the vital part of her confession. But that, queerly enough, was not what I suspected. For some reason I felt her to be as much in the dark over the whole business as I was; and that added to the strangeness of my dilemma.

"Do you know in the least what you're going for?" I asked at length.

"No, no, no--but come!"

"If he's there, he'll kick us out, most likely; kick *me* out, at any rate."

She did not answer; I saw that in her anguish she was past speaking. "Wait till I get my coat," I said.

She took my arm, and side by side we hurried in the rain through the shuttered village. As we passed the Selwick house I saw a light burning in old Miss Selwick's bedroom window. It was on the tip of my tongue to say: "Hadn't we better stop and ask Aunt Lucilla what's wrong? She knows more about Cranch than any of us!"

Then I remembered Cranch's expression the last time Aunt Lucilla's legend of the hobby-horse had been mentioned before him--the day we were planning the jumble sale--and a sudden shiver checked my pleasantry. "He looked then as he did when he passed me in the doorway yesterday," I thought; and I had a vision of my ancient relative, sitting there propped up in her bed and looking quietly into the unknown while all the village slept. Was she aware, I wondered, that we were passing under her window at that moment, and did she know what would await us when we reached our destination?

CHAPTER V

Mrs. Durant, in her thin slippers, splashed on beside me through the mud.

"Oh," she exclaimed, stopping short with a gasp, "look at the lights!"

We had crossed the green, and were groping our way under the dense elm-shadows, and there before us stood the Cranch house, all its windows illuminated. It was the only house in the village except Miss Selwick's that was not darkened and shuttered.

"Well, he can't be gone; he's giving a party, you see," I said derisively.

My companion made no answer. She only pulled me forward, and yielding once more I pushed open the tall entrance gates. In the brick path I paused. "Do you still want to go in?" I asked.

"More than ever!" She kept her tight clutch on my arm, and I walked up the path at her side and rang the bell.

The sound went on jangling for a long time through the stillness; but no one came to the door. At length Mrs. Durant laid an impatient hand on the door-panel. "But it's open!" she exclaimed.

It was probably the first time since Waldo Cranch had come back to live in the house that unbidden visitors had been free to enter it. We looked at each other in surprise and

I followed Mrs. Durant into the lamplit hall. It was empty.

With a common accord we stood for a moment listening; but not a sound came to us, though the doors of library and drawing-room stood open, and there were lighted lamps in both rooms.

"It's queer," I said, "all these lights, and no one about."

My companion had walked impulsively into the drawing-room and stood looking about at its familiar furniture. From the panelled wall, distorted by the wavering lamp-light, the old Spanish ancestress glared down duskily at us out of the shadows. Mrs. Durant had stopped short--a sound of voices, agitated, discordant, a strange man's voice among them, came to us from across the hall. Silently we retraced our steps, opened the dining-room door, and went in. But here also we found emptiness; the talking came from beyond, came, as we now perceived, from the wing which none of us had ever entered. Again we hesitated and looked at each other. Then "Come!" said Mrs. Durant in a resolute tone; and again I followed her.

She led the way into a large pantry, airy, orderly, well-stocked with china and glass. That too was empty; and two doors opened from it. Mrs. Durant passed through the one on the right, and we found ourselves, not, as I had expected, in the kitchen, but in a kind of vague unfurnished anteroom. The quarrelling voices had meanwhile died out; we seemed once more to have the mysterious place to ourselves. Suddenly, beyond another closed door, we heard a shrill crowing laugh. Mrs. Durant dashed at this last door and it let us into a large high-studded room. We paused and looked about us. Evidently we were in what Cranch had always described as the lumber-room on the ground floor of the wing. But there was no lumber in it now. It was scrupulously neat, and fitted up like a big and rather bare nursery; and in the middle of the floor, on a square of drugget, stood a great rearing black and white animal: my Aunt Lucilla's hobby-horse...

I gasped at the sight; but in spite of its strangeness it did not detain me long, for at the farther end of the room, before a fire protected by a tall nursery fender, I had seen something stranger still. Two little boys in old-fashioned round jackets and knickerbockers knelt by the hearth, absorbed in the building of a house of blocks. Mrs. Durant saw them at the same moment. She caught my arm as if she were about to fall, and uttered a faint cry.

The sound, low as it was, produced a terrifying effect on the two children. Both of them dropped their blocks, turned around as if to dart at us, and then stopped short, holding each other by the hand, and staring and trembling as if we had been ghosts.

At the opposite end of the room, we stood staring and trembling also; for it was they who were the ghosts to our terrified eyes. It must have been Mrs. Durant who spoke first.

"Oh...the poor things..." she said in a low choking voice.

The little boys stood there, motionless and far off, among the ruins of their house of blocks. But, as my eyes grew used to the faint light--there was only one lamp in the big room--and as my shaken nerves adjusted themselves to the strangeness of the scene, I perceived the meaning of Mrs. Durant's cry.

The children before us were not children; they were two tiny withered men, with frowning foreheads under their baby curls, and heavy-shouldered middle-aged bodies. The sight was horrible, and rendered more so by the sameness of their size and by their old-fashioned childish dress. I recoiled; but Mrs. Durant had let my arm go, and was moving softly forward. Her own arms outstretched, she advanced toward the two strange beings. "You poor poor things, you," she repeated, the tears running down her face.

I thought her tender tone must have drawn the little creatures; but as she advanced they continued to stand motionless, and then suddenly--each with the same small falsetto scream--turned and dashed toward the door. As they reached it, old Catherine appeared and held out her arms to them.

"Oh, my God--how dare you, madam? My young gentlemen!" she cried.

They hid their dreadful little faces in the folds of her skirt, and kneeling down she put her arms about them and received them on her bosom. Then, slowly, she lifted up her head and looked at us.

I had always, like the rest of Harpledon, thought of Catherine as a morose old Englishwoman, civil enough in her cold way, but yet forbidding. Now it seemed to me that her worn brown face, in its harsh folds of gray hair, was the saddest I had ever looked upon.

"How could you, madam; oh, how could you? Haven't we got enough else to bear?" she asked, speaking low above the cowering heads on her breast. Her eyes were on Mrs. Durant.

The latter, white and trembling, gave back the look. "Enough else? Is there *more*, then?"

"There's everything--." The old servant got to her feet, keeping her two charges by the hand. She put her finger to her lips, and stooped again to the dwarfs. "Master Waldo, Master Donald, you'll come away now with your old Catherine. No one's going to harm us, my dears; you'll just go upstairs and let Janey Sampson put you to bed, for it's very late; and presently Catherine'll come up and hear your prayers like every night." She moved to the door; but one of the dwarfs hung back, his forehead puckering, his eyes still fixed on Mrs. Durant in indescribable horror.

"Good Dobbin," cried he abruptly, in a piercing pipe.

"No, dear, no; the lady won't touch good Dobbin," said Catherine. "It's the young gentlemen's great pet," she added, glancing at the Roman steed in the middle of the floor. She led the changelings away, and a moment later returned. Her face was ashen-white under its swarthiness, and she stood looking at us like a figure of doom.

"And now, perhaps," she said, "you'll be good enough to go away too."

"Go away?" Mrs. Durant, instead, came closer to her. "How can I--when I've just had this from your master?" She held out the letter she had brought to my house.

Catherine glanced coldly at the page and returned it to her.

"He says he's going on a journey. Well, he's been, madam; been and come back," she said.

"Come back? Already? He's in the house, then? Oh, do let me--" Mrs. Durant dropped back before the old woman's frozen gaze.

"He's lying overhead, dead on his bed, madam--just as they carried him up from the beach. Do you suppose, else, you'd have ever got in here and seen the young gentlemen? He rushed out and died sooner than have them seen, the poor lambs; him that was their father, madam. And here you and this gentleman come thrusting yourselves in..."

I thought Mrs. Durant would reel under the shock; but she stood quiet, very quiet--it was almost as if the blow had mysteriously strengthened her.

"He's dead? He's killed himself?" She looked slowly about

the trivial tragic room. "Oh, now I understand," she said.

Old Catherine faced her with grim lips. "It's a pity you didn't understand sooner, then; you and the others, whoever they was, forever poking and prying; till at last that miserable girl brought in the police on us--"

"The police?"

"They was here, madam, in this house, not an hour ago, frightening my young gentlemen out of their senses. When word came that my master had been found on the beach they went down there to bring him back. Now they've gone to Hingham to report his death to the coroner. But there's one of them in the kitchen, mounting guard. Over what, I wonder? As if my young gentlemen could run away! Where in God's pity would they go? Wherever it is, I'll go with them; I'll never leave them...And here we were at peace for thirty years, till you brought that man to draw the pictures of the house..."

For the first time Mrs. Durant's strength seemed to fail her; her body drooped, and she leaned her weight against the door. She and the housekeeper stood confronted, two stricken old women staring at each other; then Mrs. Durant's agony broke from her. "Don't say I did it--don't say that!"

But the other was relentless. As she faced us, her arms outstretched, she seemed still to be defending her two charges. "What else would you have me say, madam? You brought that man here, didn't you? And he was determined

64

to see the other side of the wing, and my poor master was determined he shouldn't." She turned to me for the first time. "It was plain enough to you, sir, wasn't it? To me it was, just coming and going with the tea-things. And the minute your backs was turned, Mr. Cranch rang, and gave me the order: 'That man's never to set foot here again, you understand.' And I went out and told the other three; the cook, and Janey, and Hannah Oast, the parlour-maid. I was as sure of the cook and Janey as I was of myself; but Hannah was new, she hadn't been with us not above a year, and though I knew all about her, and had made sure before she came that she was a decent close-mouthed girl, and one that would respect our...our misfortune...yet I couldn't feel as safe about her as the others, and of her temper I wasn't sure from the first. I told Mr. Cranch so, often enough; I said: 'Remember, now, sir, not to put her pride up, won't you?' For she was jealous, and angry, I think, at never being allowed to see the young gentlemen, yet knowing they were there, as she had to know. But their father would never have any but me and Janey Sampson about them.

"Well--and then, in he came yesterday with those accursed pictures. And however had the man got in? And where was Hannah? And it must have been her doing...and swearing and cursing at her...and me crying to him and saying: 'For God's sake, sir, let be, let be...don't stir the matter up...just let me talk to her...And I went in to my little boys, to see about their supper; and before I was back, I heard a trunk bumping down the stairs, and the gardener's lad outside with a wheelbarrow, and Hannah Oast walking away out of the gate like a ramrod. 'Oh, sir, what have you done? Let me go after her!' I begged and besought him; but my master, very pale, but as calm as possible, held me back by the arm, and said: 'Don't you worry, Catherine. It passed off very quietly. We'll have no trouble from her.' 'No trouble, sir, from Hannah Oast? Oh, for pity's sake, call her back and let me smooth it over, sir!' But the girl was gone, and he wouldn't leave go of my arm nor yet listen to me, but stood there like a marble stone and saw her drive away, and wouldn't stop her. 'I'd die first, Catherine,' he said, his kind face all changed to me, and looking like that old Spanish she-devil on the parlour wall, that brought the curse on us...And this morning the police came. The gardener got wind of it, and let us know they was on the way; and my master sat and wrote a long time in his room, and then walked out, looking very quiet, and saying to me he was going to the post office, and would be back before they got here. And the next we knew of him was when they carried him up to his bed just now...And perhaps we'd best give thanks that he's at rest in it. But, oh, my young gentlemen...my young gentlemen!"

CHAPTER VI

I never saw the "young gentlemen" again. I suppose most men are cowards about calamities of that sort, the irremediable kind that have to be faced anew every morning. It takes a woman to shoulder such a lasting tragedy, and hug it to her...as I had seen Catherine doing; as I saw Mrs. Durant yearning to do...

It was about that very matter that I interviewed the old housekeeper the day after the funeral. Among the papers which the police found on poor Cranch's desk was a letter addressed to me. Like his message to Mrs. Durant it was of the briefest. "I have appointed no one to care for my sons; I expected to outlive them. Their mother would have wished Catherine to stay with them. Will you try to settle all this mercifully? There is plenty of money, but my brain won't work. Good-bye."

It was a matter, first of all, for the law; but before we entered on that phase I wanted to have a talk with old Catherine. She came to me, very decent in her new black; I hadn't the heart to go to that dreadful house again, and I think perhaps it was easier for her to speak out under another roof. At any rate, I soon saw that, after all the years of silence, speech was a relief; as it might have been to him too, poor fellow, if only he had dared! But he couldn't; there was that pride of his, his "Spanish pride" as she called it.

"Not but what he would have hated me to say so, sir; for the Spanish blood in him, and all that went with it, was what he most abominated...But there it was, closer to him than his marrow...Oh, what that old woman done to us! He told me why, once, long ago--it was about the time when he began to understand that our little boys were never going to grow up like other young gentlemen. 'It's her doing, the devil,' he said to me; and then he told me how she'd been a great Spanish heiress, a rich merchant's daughter, and had been promised, in that foreign way they have, to a young nobleman who'd never set eyes on her; and when the bridegroom came to the city where she lived, and saw her sitting in her father's box across the theatre, he turned about and mounted his horse and rode off the same night; and never a word came from him--the shame of it! It nigh killed her, I believe, and she swore then and there she'd marry a foreigner and leave Spain; and that was how she took up with young Mr. Cranch that was in her father's bank; and the old gentleman put a big sum into the Cranch shipping business, and packed off the young couple to Harpledon...But the poor misbuilt thing, it seems, couldn't ever rightly get over the hurt to her pride, nor get used to the cold climate, and the snow and the strange faces; she would go about pining for the orange-flowers and the sunshine; and though she brought her husband a son, I do believe she hated him, and was glad to die and get out of Harpledon...That was my Mr. Cranch's story...

"Well, sir, he despised his great-grandfather more than he hated the Spanish woman. 'Marry that twisted stick for her money, and put her poisoned blood in us I' He used to put it that way, sir, in his bad moments. And when he was twenty-one, and travelling abroad, he met the young English lady I was maid to, the loveliest soundest young creature you ever set eyes on. They loved and married, and the next year--oh, the pity--the next year she brought him our young gentlemen...twins, they were...When she died, a few weeks after, he was desperate...more desperate than I've ever seen him till the other day. But as the years passed, and he began to understand about our little boys--well, then he was thankful she was gone. And that thankfulness was the bitterest part of his grief.

"It was when they was about nine or ten that *he* first saw it; though I'd been certain long before that. We were living in Italy then. And one day--oh, what a day, sir!--he got a letter, Mr. Cranch did, from a circus-man who'd heard somehow of our poor little children...Oh, sir!...Then it was that he decided to leave Europe, and come back to Harpledon to live. It was a lonely lost place at that time; and there was all the big wing for our little gentlemen. We were happy in the old house, in our way; but it was a solitary life for so young a man as Mr. Cranch was then, and when the summer folk began to settle here I was glad of it, and I said to him: 'You go out, sir, now, and make friends, and invite your friends here. I'll see to it that our secret is kept.' And so I did, sir, so I did...and he always trusted me. He needed life and company himself; but he would never separate himself from the little boys. He was so proud--and yet so soft-hearted! And where could he have put the little things? They never grew past their toys--there's the worst of it. Heaps and heaps of them he brought home to them, year after year. Pets he tried too...but animals were afraid of them--just as I expect you were, sir, when you saw them," she added suddenly, "but with no reason; there were never gentler beings. Little Waldo especially--it's as if they were trying to make up for being a burden...Oh, for pity's sake, let them stay on in their father's house, and me with them, won't you, sir?"

As she wished it, so it was. The legal side of the matter did not take long to settle, for the Cranches were almost extinct; there were only some distant cousins, long since gone from Harpledon. Old Catherine was suffered to remain on with her charges in the Cranch house, and one of the guardians appointed by the courts was Mrs. Durant.

Would you have believed it? She wanted it--the horror, the responsibility and all. After that she lived all the year round at Harpledon; I believe she saw Cranch's sons every day. I never went back there; but she used sometimes to come up and see me in Boston. The first time she appeared--it must have been about a year after the events I have related--I scarcely knew her when she walked into my library. She was an old bent woman; her white hair now seemed an attribute of age, not a form of coquetry. After that, each time I saw her she seemed older and more bowed. But she told me once she was not unhappy--"not as unhappy as I used to be," she added, qualifying the phrase.

On the same occasion--it was only a few months ago--she also told me that one of the twins was ill. She did not think he would last long, she said; and old Catherine did not think so either. "It's little Waldo; he was the one who felt his father's death the most; the dark one; I really think he understands. And when he goes, Donald won't last long either." Her eyes filled with tears. "Presently I shall be alone again," she added.

I asked her then how old they were; and she thought for a moment, murmuring the years over slowly under her breath. "Only forty-one," she said at length--as if she had said "Only four."

Women are strange. I am their other guardian; and I have never yet had the courage to go down to Harpledon and see them.

BEWITCHED

CHAPTER I

The snow was still falling thickly when Orrin Bosworth, who farmed the land south of Lone-top, drove up in his cutter to Saul Rutledge's gate. He was surprised to see two other cutters ahead of him. From them descended two muffled figures. Bosworth, with increasing surprise, recognized Deacon Hibben, from North Ashmore, and Sylvester Brand, the widower, from the old Bearcliff farm on the way to Lonetop.

It was not often that anybody in Hemlock County entered Saul Rutledge's gate; least of all in the dead of winter, and summoned (as Bosworth, at any rate, had been) by Mrs. Rutledge, who passed, even in that unsocial region, for a woman of cold manners and solitary character. The situation was enough to excite the curiosity of a less imaginative man than Orrin Bosworth.

As he drove in between the broken-down white gate-posts topped by fluted urns the two men ahead of him were leading their horses to the adjoining shed. Bosworth followed, and hitched his horse to a post. Then the three tossed off the snow from their shoulders, clapped their numb hands together, and greeted each other.

"Hallo, Deacon."

"Well, well, Orrin--." They shook hands.

"'Day, Bosworth," said Sylvester Brand, with a brief nod. He seldom put any cordiality into his manner, and on this occasion he was still busy about his horse's bridle and blanket.

Orrin Bosworth, the youngest and most communicative of the three, turned back to Deacon Hibben, whose long face, queerly blotched and mouldy-looking, with blinking peering eyes, was yet less forbidding than Brand's heavily-hewn countenance.

"Queer, our all meeting here this way. Mrs. Rutledge sent me a message to come," Bosworth volunteered.

The Deacon nodded. "I got a word from her too--Andy Pond come with it yesterday noon. I hope there's no trouble here--"

He glanced through the thickening fall of snow at the desolate front of the Rutledge house, the more melancholy in its present neglected state because, like the gate-posts, it kept traces of former elegance. Bosworth had often wondered how such a house had come to be built in that lonely stretch between North Ashmore and Cold Corners. People said there had once been other houses like it, forming a little township called Ashmore, a sort of mountain colony created by the caprice of an English Royalist officer, one Colonel Ashmore, who had been murdered by the Indians, with all his family, long before the Revolution. This tale was confirmed by the fact that the ruined cellars of several smaller houses were still to be discovered under the wild growth of the adjoining slopes, and that the Communion plate of the moribund Episcopal church of Cold Corners was engraved with the name of Colonel Ashmore, who had given it to the church of Ashmore in the year 1723. Of the church itself no traces remained. Doubtless it had been a modest wooden edifice, built on piles, and the conflagration which had burnt the other houses to the ground's edge had reduced it utterly to ashes. The whole place, even in summer, wore a mournful solitary air, and people wondered why Saul Rutledge's father had gone there to settle.

"I never knew a place," Deacon Hibben said, "as seemed as far away from humanity. And yet it ain't so in miles."

"Miles ain't the only distance," Orrin Bosworth answered; and the two men, followed by Sylvester Brand, walked across the drive to the front door. People in Hemlock County did not usually come and go by their front doors, but all three men seemed to feel that, on an occasion which appeared to be so exceptional, the usual and more familiar approach by the kitchen would not be suitable.

They had judged rightly; the Deacon had hardly lifted the knocker when the door opened and Mrs. Rutledge stood before them.

"Walk right in," she said in her usual dead-level tone; and Bosworth, as he followed the others, thought to himself;

"Whatever's happened, she's not going to let it show in her face."

It was doubtful, indeed, if anything unwonted could be made to show in Prudence Rutledge's face, so limited was its scope, so fixed were its features. She was dressed for the occasion in a black calico with white spots, a collar of crochet-lace fastened by a gold brooch, and a gray woollen shawl crossed under her arms and tied at the back. In her small narrow head the only marked prominence was that of the brow projecting roundly over pale spectacled eyes. Her dark hair, parted above this prominence, passed tight and fiat over the tips of her ears into a small braided coil at the nape; and her contracted head looked still narrower from being perched on a long hollow neck with cord-like throat-muscles. Her eyes were of a pale cold gray, her complexion was an even white. Her age might have been anywhere from thirty-five to sixty.

The room into which she led the three men had probably been the dining-room of the Ashmore house. It was now used as a front parlour, and a black stove planted on a sheet of zinc stuck out from the delicately fluted panels of an old wooden mantel. A newly-lit fire smouldered reluctantly, and the room was at once close and bitterly cold.

"Andy Pond," Mrs. Rutledge cried to some one at the back of the house, "step out and call Mr. Rutledge. You'll likely find him in the wood-shed, or round the barn somewheres."

She rejoined her visitors. "Please suit yourselves to seats," she said.

The three men, with an increasing air of constraint, took the chairs she pointed out, and Mrs. Rutledge sat stiffly down upon a fourth, behind a rickety bead-work table. She glanced from one to the other of her visitors.

"I presume you folks are wondering what it is I asked you to come here for," she said in her dead-level voice. Orrin Bosworth and Deacon Hibben murmured an assent; Sylvester Brand sat silent, his eyes, under their great thicket of eyebrows, fixed on the huge boot-tip swinging before him.

"Well, I allow you didn't expect it was for a party," continued Mrs. Rutledge.

No one ventured to respond to this chill pleasantry, and she continued: "We're in trouble here, and that's the fact. And we need advice--Mr. Rutledge and myself do." She cleared her throat, and added in a lower tone, her pitilessly clear eyes looking straight before her: "There's a spell been cast over Mr. Rutledge."

The Deacon looked up sharply, an incredulous smile pinching his thin lips. "A spell?"

"That's what I said: he's bewitched."

Again the three visitors were silent; then Bosworth, more at ease or less tongue-tied than the others, asked with an attempt at humour: "Do you use the word in the strict

Scripture sense, Mrs. Rutledge?"

She glanced at him before replying: "That's how *he* uses it."

The Deacon coughed and cleared his long rattling throat. "Do you care to give us more particulars before your husband joins us?"

Mrs. Rutledge looked down at her clasped hands, as if considering the question. Bosworth noticed that the inner fold of her lids was of the same uniform white as the rest of her skin, so that when she dropped them her rather prominent eyes looked like the sightless orbs of a marble statue. The impression was unpleasing, and he glanced away at the text over the mantelpiece, which read:

The Soul That Sinneth It Shall Die.

"No," she said at length, "I'll wait."

At this moment Sylvester Brand suddenly stood up and pushed back his chair. "I don't know," he said, in his rough bass voice, "as I've got any particular lights on Bible mysteries; and this happens to be the day I was to go down to Starkfield to close a deal with a man."

Mrs. Rutledge lifted one of her long thin hands. Withered and wrinkled by hard work and cold, it was nevertheless of the same leaden white as her face. "You won't be kept long," she said. "Won't you be seated?"

Farmer Brand stood irresolute, his purplish underlip twitching. "The Deacon here---such things is more in his line..."

"I want you should stay," said Mrs. Rutledge quietly; and Brand sat down again.

A silence fell, during which the four persons present seemed all to be listening for the sound of a step; but none was heard, and after a minute or two Mrs. Rutledge began to speak again.

"It's down by that old shack on Lamer's pond; that's where they meet," she said suddenly.

Bosworth, whose eyes were on Sylvester Brand's face, fancied he saw a sort of inner flush darken the farmer's heavy leathern skin. Deacon Hibben leaned forward, a glitter of curiosity in his eyes.

"They--*who*, Mrs. Rutledge?"

"My husband, Saul Rutledge...and her..."

Sylvester Brand again stirred in his seat. "Who do you mean by *her*?" he asked abruptly, as if roused out of some far-off musing.

Mrs. Rutledge's body did not move; she simply revolved her head on her long neck and looked at him.

"Your daughter, Sylvester Brand."

The man staggered to his feet with an explosion of inarticulate sounds. "My--my daughter? What the hell are you talking about? My daughter? It's a damned lie...it's... it's..."

"Your daughter *Ora*, Mr. Brand," said Mrs. Rutledge

slowly.

Bosworth felt an icy chill down his spine. Instinctively he turned his eyes away from Brand, and, they rested on the mildewed countenance of Deacon Hibben. Between the blotches it had become as white as Mrs. Rutledge's, and the Deacon's eyes burned in the whiteness like live embers among ashes.

Brand gave a laugh: the rusty creaking laugh of one whose springs of mirth are never moved by gaiety. "My daughter *Ora?*" he repeated.

"Yes."

"My *dead* daughter?"

"That's what he says."

"Your husband?"

"That's what Mr. Rutledge says."

Orrin Bosworth listened with a sense of suffocation; he felt as if he were wrestling with long-armed horrors in a dream. He could no longer resist letting his eyes return to Sylvester Brand's face. To his surprise it had resumed a natural imperturbable expression. Brand rose to his feet. "Is that all?" he queried contemptuously.

"All? Ain't it enough? How long is it since you folks seen Saul Rutledge, any of you?" Mrs. Rutledge flew out at them.

Bosworth, it appeared, had not seen him for nearly a year; the Deacon had only run across him once, for a minute, at the North Ashmore post office, the previous autumn, and acknowledged that he wasn't looking any too good then. Brand said nothing, but stood irresolute.

"Well, if you wait a minute you'll see with your own eyes; and he'll tell you with his own words. That's what I've got you here for--to see for yourselves what's come over him. Then you'll talk different," she added, twisting her head abruptly toward Sylvester Brand.

The Deacon raised a lean hand of interrogation.

"Does your husband know we've been sent for on this business, Mrs. Rutledge?" Mrs. Rutledge signed assent.

"It was with his consent, then--?"

She looked coldly at her questioner. "I guess it had to be," she said. Again Bosworth felt the chill down his spine. He tried to dissipate the sensation by speaking with an affectation of energy.

"Can you tell us, Mrs. Rutledge, how this trouble you speak of shows itself...what makes you think...?"

She looked at him for a moment; then she leaned forward across the rickety bead-work table. A thin smile of disdain narrowed her colourless lips. "I don't think--I know."

"Well--but how?"

She leaned closer, both elbows on the table, her voice dropping. "I seen 'em."

In the ashen light from the veiling of snow beyond the windows the Deacon's little screwed-up eyes seemed to give out red sparks. "Him and the dead?"

"Him and the dead."

"Saul Rutledge and--and Ora Brand?"

"That's so."

Sylvester Brand's chair fell backward with a crash. He was on his feet again, crimson and cursing. "It's a God-damned fiend-begotten lie..."

"Friend Brand...friend Brand..." the Deacon protested.

"Here, let me get out of this. I want to see Saul Rutledge himself, and tell him--"

"Well, here he is," said Mrs. Rutledge.

The outer door had opened; they heard the familiar stamping and shaking of a man who rids his garments of their last snowflakes before penetrating to the sacred precincts of the best parlour. Then Saul Rutledge entered.

CHAPTER II

As he came in he faced the light from the north window, and Bosworth's first thought was that he looked like a drowned man fished out from under the ice--"self-drowned," he added. But the snow-light plays cruel tricks with a man's colour, and even with the shape of his features; it must have been partly that, Bosworth reflected, which transformed Saul Rutledge from the straight muscular fellow he had been a year before into the haggard wretch now before them.

The Deacon sought for a word to ease the horror. "Well, now, Saul--you look's if you'd ought to set right up to the stove. Had a touch of ague, maybe?"

The feeble attempt was unavailing. Rutledge neither moved nor answered. He stood among them silent, incommunicable, like one risen from the dead.

Brand grasped him roughly by the shoulder. "See here, Saul Rutledge, what's this dirty lie your wife tells us you've been putting about?"

Still Rutledge did not move. "It's no lie," he said.

Brand's hand dropped from his shoulder. In spite of the man's rough bullying power he seemed to be undefinably awed by Rut-ledge's look and tone.

"No lie? You've gone plumb crazy, then, have you?"

Mrs. Rutledge spoke. "My husband's not lying, nor he ain't gone crazy. Don't I tell you I seen 'em?"

Brand laughed again. "Him and the dead?"

"Yes."

"Down by the Lamer pond, you say?"

"Yes."

"And when was that, if I might ask?"

"Day before yesterday."

A silence fell on the strangely assembled group. The Deacon at length broke it to say to Mr. Brand: "Brand, in my opinion we've got to see this thing through."

Brand stood for a moment in speechless contemplation: there was something animal and primitive about him, Bosworth thought, as he hung thus, lowering and dumb, a little foam beading the corners of that heavy purplish underlip. He let himself slowly down into his chair. "I'll see it through."

The two other men and Mrs. Rutledge had remained seated. Saul Rutledge stood before them, like a prisoner at the bar, or rather like a sick man before the physicians who were to heal him. As Bosworth scrutinized that hollow face, so wan under the dark sunburn, so sucked inward and consumed by some hidden fever, there stole over the sound healthy man the thought that perhaps, after all, husband and wife spoke the truth, and that they were all at that moment really standing on the edge of some forbidden mystery. Things that the rational mind would reject without a thought seemed no longer so easy to dispose of as one looked at the actual

Saul Rutledge and remembered the man he had been a year before. Yes; as the Deacon said, they would have to see it through...

"Sit down then, Saul; draw up to us, won't you?" the Deacon suggested, trying again for a natural tone.

Mrs. Rutledge pushed a chair forward, and her husband sat down on it. He stretched out his arms and grasped his knees in his brown bony fingers; in that attitude he remained, turning neither his head nor his eyes.

"Well, Saul," the Deacon continued, "your wife says you thought mebbe we could do something to help you through this trouble, whatever it is."

Rutledge's gray eyes widened a little. "No; I didn't think that. It was her idea to try what could be done."

"I presume, though, since you've agreed to our coming, that you don't object to our putting a few questions?"

Rutledge was silent for a moment; then he said with a visible effort: "No; I don't object."

"Well--you've heard what your wife says?"

Rutledge made a slight motion of assent. "And--what have you got to answer? How do you explain...?"

Mrs. Rutledge intervened. "How can he explain? I seen 'em."

There was a silence; then Bosworth, trying to speak in an easy reassuring tone, queried: "That so, Saul?"

"That's so."

Brand lifted up his brooding head. "You mean to say you... you sit here before us all and say..."

The Deacon's hand again checked him. "Hold on, friend Brand. We're all of us trying for the facts, ain't we?" He turned to Rutledge. "We've heard what Mrs. Rutledge says. What's your answer?"

"I don't know as there's any answer. She found us."

"And you mean to tell me the person with you was...was what you took to be..." the Deacon's thin voice grew thinner: "Ora Brand?"

Saul Rutledge nodded.

"You knew...or thought you knew...you were meeting with the dead?"

Rutledge bent his head again. The snow continued to fall in a steady unwavering sheet against the window, and Bosworth felt as if a winding-sheet were descending from the sky to envelop them all in a common grave.

"Think what you're saying! It's against our religion! Ora... poor child!...died over a year ago. I saw you at her funeral, Saul. How can you make such a statement?"

"What else can he do?" thrust in Mrs. Rutledge.

There was another pause. Bosworth's resources had failed him, and Brand once more sat plunged in dark meditation. The Deacon laid his quivering finger-tips together, and moistened his lips.

"Was the day before yesterday the first time?" he asked.

The movement of Rutledge's head was negative.

"Not the first? Then when..."

"Nigh on a year ago, I reckon."

"God! And you mean to tell us that ever since--?"

"Well...look at him," said his wife. The three men lowered their eyes.

After a moment Bosworth, trying to collect himself, glanced at the Deacon. "Why not ask Saul to make his own statement, if that's what we're here for?"

"That's so," the Deacon assented. He turned to Rutledge. "Will you try and give us your idea...of...of how it began?"

There was another silence. Then Rutledge tightened his grasp on his gaunt knees, and still looking straight ahead, with his curiously clear unseeing gaze: "Well," he said, "I guess it begun away back, afore even I was married to Mrs. Rutledge..." He spoke in a low automatic tone, as if some invisible agent were dictating his words, or even uttering them for him. "You know," he added, "Ora and me was to have been married."

Sylvester Brand lifted his, head. "Straighten that statement out first, please," he interjected.

"What I mean is, we kept company. But Ora she was very young. Mr. Brand here he sent her away. She was gone nigh to three years, I guess. When she come back I was married."

"That's right," Brand said, relapsing once more into his sunken attitude.

"And after she came back did you meet her again?" the Deacon continued.

"Alive?" Rutledge questioned.

A perceptible shudder ran through the room.

"Well--of course," said the Deacon nervously.

Rutledge seemed to consider. "Once I did--only once. There was a lot of other people round. At Cold Corners fair it was." "Did you talk with her then?"

"Only a minute."

"What did she say?"

His voice dropped. "She said she was sick and knew she was going to die, and when she was dead she'd come back to me."

"And what did you answer?"

"Nothing."

"Did you think anything of it at the time?"

"Well, no. Not till I heard she was dead I didn't. After that I thought of it--and I guess she drew me." He moistened his lips.

"Drew you down to that abandoned house by the pond?"

Rutledge made a faint motion of assent, and the Deacon added: "How did you know it was there she wanted you to come?"

"She...just drew me..."

There was a long pause. Bosworth felt, on himself and the other two men, the oppressive weight of the next question to be asked. Mrs. Rutledge opened and closed her narrow lips once or twice, like some beached shell-fish gasping for the tide. Rutledge waited.

"Well, now, Saul, won't you go on with what you was telling us?" the Deacon at length suggested.

"That's all. There's nothing else."

The Deacon lowered his voice. "She just draws you?"

"Yes."

"Often?"

"That's as it happens..."

"But if it's always there she draws you, man, haven't you the strength to keep away from the place?"

For the first time, Rutledge wearily turned his head toward his questioner. A spectral smile narrowed his colourless lips. "Ain't any use. She follers after me..."

There was another silence. What more could they ask, then and there? Mrs. Rut-ledge's presence checked the next question. The Deacon seemed hopelessly to revolve the matter. At length he spoke in a more authoritative tone. "These are forbidden things. You know that, Saul. Have you tried prayer?"

Rutledge shook his head.

"Will you pray with us now?"

Rutledge cast a glance of freezing indifference on his spiritual adviser. "If you folks want to pray, I'm agreeable," he said. But Mrs. Rutledge intervened.

"Prayer ain't any good. In this kind of thing it ain't no manner of use; you know it ain't. I called you here, Deacon, because you remember the last case in this parish. Thirty years ago it was, I guess; but you remember. Lefferts Nash--did praying help him? I was a little girl then, but I used to hear my folks talk of it winter nights. Lefferts Nash and Hannah Cory. They drove a stake through her breast. That's what cured him."

"Oh--" Orrin Bosworth exclaimed.

Sylvester Brand raised his head. "You're speaking of that old story as if this was the same sort of thing?"

"Ain't it? Ain't my husband pining away the same as Lefferts Nash did? The Deacon here knows--"

The Deacon stirred anxiously in his chair. "These are forbidden things," he repeated. "Supposing your husband is quite sincere in thinking himself haunted, as you might say. Well, even then, what proof have we that the...the dead woman...is the spectre of that poor girl?"

"Proof? Don't he say so? Didn't she tell him? Ain't I seen 'em?" Mrs. Rutledge almost screamed.

The three men sat silent, and suddenly the wife burst out: "A stake through the breast That's the old way; and it's the only way. The Deacon knows it!"

"It's against our religion to disturb the dead."

"Ain't it against your religion to let the living perish as my husband is perishing?" She sprang up with one of her abrupt movements and took the family Bible from the what-not in a corner of die parlour. Putting the book on the table, and moistening a livid finger-tip, she turned the pages rapidly, till she came to one on which she laid her hand like a stony paper-weight. "See here," she said, and read out in her level chanting voice:

"'*Thou shalt not suffer a witch to live.*'

"That's in Exodus, that's where it is," she added, leaving the book open as if to confirm the statement.

Bosworth continued to glance anxiously from one to the other of the four people about the table. He was younger than any of them, and had had more contact with the modern world; down in Starkfield, in the bar of the Fielding House, he could hear himself laughing with the rest of the men at such old wives' tales. But it was not for nothing that he had been born under the icy shadow of Lonetop, and had shivered and hungered as a lad through the bitter Hemlock County winters. After his parents died, and he had taken hold of the farm himself, he had got more out of it by using improved methods, and by supplying the increasing throng of summer-boarders over Stotesbury way with milk and vegetables. He had been made a selectman of North Ashmore; for so young a man he had a standing in the county. But the roots of the old life were still in him. He could remember, as a little boy, going twice a year with his mother to that bleak hill-farm out beyond Sylvester Brand's, where Mrs. Bosworth's aunt, Cressidora Cheney, had been shut up for years in a cold clean room with iron bars in the windows. When little Orrin first saw Aunt Cressidora she was a small white old woman, whom her sisters used to "make decent" for visitors the day that Orrin and his mother were expected. The child wondered why there were bars to the window. "Like a canary-bird," he said to his mother. The phrase made Mrs. Bosworth reflect. "I do believe they keep Aunt Cressidora too lonesome," she said; and the next time she went up the mountain with the little boy he carried to his great-aunt a canary in a little wooden cage. It was a great excitement; he knew it would make her happy.

The old woman's motionless face lit up when she saw the bird, and her eyes began to glitter. "It belongs to me," she said instantly, stretching her soft bony hand over the cage.

"Of course it does, Aunt Cressy," said Mrs. Bosworth, her eyes filling.

But the bird, startled by the shadow of the old woman's hand, began to flutter and beat its wings distractedly. At the sight, Aunt Cressidora's calm face suddenly became a coil of twitching features. "You she-devil, you!" she cried in a high squealing voice; and thrusting her hand into the cage she dragged out the terrified bird and wrung its neck. She was plucking the hot body, and squealing "she-devil, she-devil!" as they drew little Orrin from the room. On the way down the mountain his mother wept a great deal, and said: "You must never tell anybody that poor Auntie's crazy, or the men would come and take her down to the asylum at Starkfield, and the shame of it would kill us all. Now promise." The child promised.

He remembered the scene now, with its deep fringe of mystery, secrecy and rumour. It seemed related to a great many other things below the surface of his thoughts, things which stole up anew, making him feel that all the old people he had known, and who "believed in these things," might after all be right. Hadn't a witch been burned at North Ashmore? Didn't the summer folk still drive over in jolly buckboard loads to see the meeting-house where the trial had been held, the pond where they had ducked her and she had floated?...Deacon Hibben believed; Bosworth was sure of it. If he didn't, why did people from all over the place come to him when their animals had queer sicknesses, or when there was a child in the family that had to be kept shut up because it fell down flat and foamed? Yes, in spite of his religion, Deacon Hibben *knew*...

And Brand? Well, it came to Bosworth in a flash: that North Ashmore woman who was burned had the name of Brand. The same stock, no doubt; there had been Brands in Hemlock County ever since the white men had come there. And Orrin, when he was a child, remembered hearing his parents say that Sylvester Brand hadn't ever oughter married his own cousin, because of the blood. Yet the couple had

had two healthy girls, and when Mrs. Brand pined away and died nobody suggested that anything had been wrong with her mind. And Vanessa and Ora were the handsomest girls anywhere round. Brand knew it, and scrimped and saved all he could to send Ora, the eldest, down to Starkfield to learn book-keeping. "When she's married I'll send you," he used to say to little Venny, who was his favourite. But Ora never married. She was away three years, during which Venny ran wild on the slopes of Lonetop; and when Ora came back she sickened and died--poor girl! Since then Brand had grown more savage and morose. He was a hard-working farmer, but there wasn't much to be got out of those barren Bearcliff acres. He was said to have taken to drink since his wife's death; now and then men ran across him in the "dives" of Stotesbury. But not often. And between times he laboured hard on his stony acres and did his best for his daughters. In the neglected grave-yard of Cold Corners there was a slanting head-stone marked with his wife's name; near it, a year since, he had laid his eldest daughter. And sometimes, at dusk, in the autumn, the village people saw him walk slowly by, turn in between the graves, and stand looking down on the two stones. But he never brought a flower there, or planted a bush; nor Venny either. She was too wild and ignorant...

Mrs. Rutledge repeated: "That's in Exodus."

The three visitors remained silent, turning about their hats in reluctant hands. Rutledge faced them, still with that empty pellucid gaze which frightened Bosworth. What was he seeing?

"Ain't any of you folks got the grit--?" his wife burst out again, half hysterically.

Deacon Hibben held up his hand. "That's no way, Mrs. Rutledge. This ain't a question of having grit. What we want first of all is...proof..."

"That's so," said Bosworth, with an explosion of relief, as if the words had lifted something black and crouching from his breast. Involuntarily the eyes of both men had turned to Brand. He stood there smiling grimly, but did not speak.

"Ain't it so, Brand?" the Deacon prompted him.

"Proof that spooks walk?" the other sneered.

"Well--I presume you want this business settled too?"

The old farmer squared his shoulders. "Yes--I do. But I ain't a sperritualist. How the hell are you going to settle it?"

Deacon Hibben hesitated; then he said, in a low incisive tone: "I don't see but one way--Mrs. Rutledge's."

There was a silence.

"What?" Brand sneered again. "Spying?"

The Deacon's voice sank lower. "If the poor girl *does* walk... her that's your child...wouldn't you be the first to want her laid quiet? We all know there've been such cases...mysterious visitations...Can any one of us here deny it?"

"I seen 'em," Mrs. Rutledge interjected.

There was another heavy pause. Suddenly Brand fixed his

gaze on Rutledge. "See here, Saul Rutledge, you've got to clear up this damned calumny, or I'll know why. You say my dead girl comes to you." He laboured with his breath, and then jerked out: "When? You tell me that, and I'll be there."

Rutledge's head drooped a little, and his eyes wandered to the window. "Round about sunset, mostly."

"You know beforehand?"

Rutledge made a sign of assent.

"Well, then--tomorrow, will it be?" Rutledge made the same sign.

Brand turned to the door. "I'll be there." That was all he said. He strode out between them without another glance or word. Deacon Hibben looked at Mrs. Rutledge. "We'll be there too," he said, as if she had asked him; but she had not spoken, and Bosworth saw that her thin body was trembling all over. He was glad when he and Hibben were out again in the snow.

CHAPTER III

They thought that Brand wanted to be left to himself, and to give him time to unhitch his horse they made a pretense of hanging about in the doorway while Bosworth searched his pockets for a pipe he had no mind to light.

But Brand turned back to them as they lingered. "You'll meet me down by Lamer's pond tomorrow?" he suggested. "I want witnesses. Round about sunset."

They nodded their acquiescence, and he got into his sleigh, gave the horse a cut across the flanks, and drove off under the snow-smothered hemlocks. The other two men went to the shed.

"What do you make of this business, Deacon?" Bosworth asked, to break the silence.

The Deacon shook his head. "The man's a sick man--that's sure. Something's sucking the life clean out of him."

But already, in the biting outer air, Bosworth was getting himself under better control. "Looks to me like a bad case of the ague, as you said."

"Well--ague of the mind, then. It's his brain that's sick."

Bosworth shrugged. "He ain't the first in Hemlock County."

CHAPTER IV

"That's so," the Deacon agreed. "It's a worm in the brain, solitude is."

"Well, we'll know this time tomorrow, maybe," said Bosworth. He scrambled into his sleigh, and was driving off in his turn when he heard his companion calling after him. The Deacon explained that his horse had cast a shoe; would Bosworth drive him down to the forge near North Ashmore, if it wasn't too much out of his way? He didn't want the mare slipping about on the freezing snow, and he could probably get the blacksmith to drive him back and shoe her in Rutledge's shed. Bosworth made room for him under the bearskin, and the two men drove off, pursued by a puzzled whinny from the Deacon's old mare.

The road they took was not the one that Bosworth would have followed to reach his own home. But he did not mind that. The shortest way to the forge passed close by Lamer's pond, and Bosworth, since he was in for the business, was not sorry to look the ground over. They drove on in silence.

The snow had ceased, and a green sunset was spreading upward into the crystal sky. A stinging wind barbed with ice-flakes caught them in the face on the open ridges, but when they dropped down into the hollow by Lamer's pond the air was as soundless and empty as an unswung bell. They jogged along slowly, each thinking his own thoughts.

"That's the house...that tumble-down shack over there, I suppose?" the Deacon said, as the road drew near the edge of the frozen pond.

"Yes: that's the house. A queer hermit-fellow built it years ago, my father used to tell me. Since then I don't believe it's ever been used but by the gipsies."

Bosworth had reined in his horse, and sat looking through pine-trunks purpled by the sunset at the crumbling structure. Twilight already lay under the trees, though day lingered in the open. Between two sharply-patterned pine-boughs he saw the evening star, like a white boat in a sea of green.

His gaze dropped from that fathomless sky and followed the blue-white undulations of the snow. It gave him a curious agitated feeling to think that here, in this icy solitude, in the tumble-down house he had so often passed without heeding it, a dark mystery, too deep for thought, was being enacted. Down that very slope, coming from the grave-yard at Cold Corners, the being they called "Ora" must pass toward the pond. His heart began to beat stiflingly. Suddenly he gave an exclamation: "Look!"

He had jumped out of the cutter and was stumbling up the bank toward the slope of snow. On it, turned in the direction of the house by the pond, he had detected a woman's footprints; two; then three; then more. The Deacon scrambled out after him, and they stood and stared.

"God--barefoot!" Hibben gasped. "Then it *is*...the dead..."

Bosworth said nothing. But he knew that no live woman would travel with naked feet across that freezing wilderness. Here, then, was the proof the Deacon had asked for--they held it. What should they do with it?

"Supposing we was to drive up nearer--round the turn of the pond, till we get close to the house," the Deacon proposed in a colourless voice. "Mebbe then..."

Postponement was a relief. They got into the sleigh and drove on. Two or three hundred yards farther the road, a mere lane under steep bushy banks, turned sharply to the right, following the bend of the pond. As they rounded the turn they saw Brand's cutter ahead of them. It was empty, the horse tied to a tree-trunk. The two men looked at each other again. This was not Brand's nearest way home.

Evidently he had been actuated by the same impulse which had made them rein in their horse by the pond-side, and then hasten on to the deserted hovel. Had he too discovered those spectral foot-prints? Perhaps it was for that very reason that he had left his cutter and vanished in the direction of the house. Bosworth found himself shivering all over under his bearskin. "I wish to God the dark wasn't coming on," he muttered. He tethered his own horse near Brand's, and without a word he and the Deacon ploughed through the snow, in the track of Brand's huge feet. They had only a few yards to walk to overtake him. He did not hear them following him, and when Bosworth spoke his name, and he stopped short and turned, his heavy face was dim and confused, like a darker blot on the dusk. He looked at them dully, but without surprise.

"I wanted to see the place," he merely said.

The Deacon cleared his throat. "Just take a look...yes...We thought so...But I guess there won't be anything to *see*..." He attempted a chuckle.

The other did not seem to hear him, but laboured on ahead through the pines. The three men came out together in the cleared space before the house. As they emerged from beneath the trees they seemed to have left night behind. The evening star shed a lustre on the speckless snow, and Brand, in that lucid circle, stopped with a jerk, and pointed to the same light foot-prints turned toward the house--the track of a woman in the snow. He stood still, his face working. "Bare feet..." he said.

The Deacon piped up in a quavering voice: "The feet of the dead."

Brand remained motionless. "The feet of the dead," he echoed.

Deacon Hibben laid a frightened hand on his arm. "Come away now, Brand; for the love of God come away."

The father hung there, gazing down at those light tracks on the snow--light as fox or squirrel trails they seemed, on the white immensity. Bosworth thought to himself "The living couldn't walk so light--not even Ora Brand couldn't have, when she lived..." The cold seemed to have entered into his very marrow. His teeth were chattering.

Brand swung about on them abruptly. "*Now!*" he said, moving on as if to an assault, his head bowed forward on his bull neck.

"Now--now? Not in there?" gasped the Deacon. "What's the use? It was tomorrow he said--." He shook like a leaf.

"It's now," said Brand. He went up to the door of the crazy house, pushed it inward, and meeting with an unexpected resistance, thrust his heavy shoulder against the panel. The door collapsed like a playing-card, and Brand stumbled after it into the darkness of the hut. The others, after a moment's hesitation, followed.

Bosworth was never quite sure in what order the events that succeeded took place. Coming in out of the snow-dazzle, he seemed to be plunging into total blackness. He groped his way across the threshold, caught a sharp splinter of the fallen door in his palm, seemed to see something white and wraithlike surge up out of the darkest corner of the hut, and then heard a revolver shot at his elbow, and a cry--

Brand had turned back, and was staggering past him out into the lingering daylight. The sunset, suddenly flushing through the trees, crimsoned his face like blood. He held a revolver in his hand and looked about him in his stupid way.

"They *do* walk, then," he said and began to laugh. He bent

101

his head to examine his weapon. "Better here than in the churchyard. They shan't dig her up *now*," he shouted out. The two men caught him by the arms, and Bosworth got the revolver away from him.

CHAPTER V

The next day Bosworth's sister Loretta, who kept house for him, asked him, when he came in for his midday dinner, if he had heard the news.

Bosworth had been sawing wood all the morning, and in spite of the cold and the driving snow, which had begun again in the night, he was covered with an icy sweat, like a man getting over a fever.

"What news?"

"Venny Brand's down sick with pneumonia. The Deacon's been there. I guess she's dying."

Bosworth looked at her with listless eyes. She seemed far off from him, miles away. "Venny Brand?" he echoed.

"You never liked her, Orrin."

"She's a child. I never knew much about her."

"Well," repeated his sister, with the guileless relish of the unimaginative for bad news, "I guess she's dying." After a pause she added: "It'll kill Sylvester Brand, all alone up there."

Bosworth got up and said: "I've got to see to poulticing the gray's fetlock." He walked out into the steadily falling snow.

Venny Brand was buried three days later. The Deacon read the service; Bosworth was one of the pall-bearers. The whole countryside turned out, for the snow had stopped falling, and at any season a funeral offered an opportunity for an outing that was not to be missed. Besides, Venny Brand was young and handsome--at least some people thought her handsome, though she was so swarthy--and her dying like that, so suddenly, had the fascination of tragedy.

"They say her lungs filled right up...Seems she'd had bronchial troubles before...I always said both them girls was frail...Look at Ora, how she took and wasted away I And it's colder'n all outdoors up there to Brand's...Their mother, too, *she* pined away just the same. They don't ever make old bones on the mother's side of the family...There's that young Bedlow over there; they say Venny was engaged to him...Oh, Mrs. Rutledge, excuse *me*...Step right into the pew; there's a seat for you alongside of grandma..."

Mrs. Rutledge was advancing with deliberate step down the narrow aisle of the bleak wooden church. She had on her best bonnet, a monumental structure which no one had seen out of her trunk since old Mrs. Silsee's funeral, three years before. All the women remembered it. Under its perpendicular pile her narrow face, swaying on the long thin neck, seemed whiter than ever; but her air of fretfulness had been composed into a suitable expression of mournful immobility.

"Looks as if the stone-mason had carved her to put atop of Venny's grave," Bosworth thought as she glided past him; and then shivered at his own sepulchral fancy. When she bent over her hymn book her lowered lids reminded him again of marble eye-balls; the bony hands clasping the book were bloodless. Bosworth had never seen such hands since he had seen old Aunt Cressidora Cheney strangle the canary-bird because it fluttered.

The service was over, the coffin of Venny Brand had been lowered into her sister's grave, and the neighbours were slowly dispersing. Bosworth, as pall-bearer, felt obliged to linger and say a word to the stricken father. He waited till Brand had turned from the grave with the Deacon at his side. The three men stood together for a moment; but not one of them spoke. Brand's face was the closed door of a vault, barred with wrinkles like bands of iron.

Finally the Deacon took his hand and said: "The Lord gave--"

Brand nodded and turned away toward the shed where the horses were hitched. Bosworth followed him. "Let me drive along home with you," he suggested.

Brand did not so much as turn his head. "Home? What home?" he said; and the other fell back.

Loretta Bosworth was talking with the other women while the men unblanketed their horses and backed the cutters out into the heavy snow. As Bosworth waited for her, a few feet off, he saw Mrs. Rutledge's tall bonnet lording it above the group. Andy Pond, the Rutledge farm-hand, was backing out the sleigh.

"Saul ain't here today, Mrs. Rutledge, is he?" one of the

village elders piped, turning a benevolent old tortoise-head about on a loose neck, and blinking up into Mrs. Rut-ledge's marble face.

Bosworth heard her measure out her answer in slow incisive words. "No. Mr. Rutledge he ain't here. He would 'a' come for certain, but his aunt Minorca Cummins is being buried down to Stotesbury this very day and he had to go down there. Don't it sometimes seem zif we was all walking right in the Shadow of Death?"

As she walked toward the cutter, in which Andy Pond was already seated, the Deacon went up to her with visible hesitation. Involuntarily Bosworth also moved nearer. He heard the Deacon say: "I'm glad to hear that Saul is able to be up and around."

She turned her small head on her rigid neck, and lifted the lids of marble.

"Yes, I guess he'll sleep quieter now.--And her too, maybe, now she don't lay there alone any longer," she added in a low voice, with a sudden twist of her chin toward the fresh black stain in the grave-yard snow. She got into the cutter, and said in a clear tone to Andy Pond: "'S long as we're down here I don't know but what I'll just call round and get a box of soap at Hiram Pringle's."

THE SEED OF THE FAITH

CHAPTER I

The blinding June sky of Africa hung over the town. In the doorway of an Arab coffee-house a young man stood listening to the remarks exchanged by the patrons of the establishment, who lay in torpid heaps on the low shelf bordering the room.

The young man's caftan was faded to a dingy brown, but the muslin garment covering it was clean, and so was the turban wound about his shabby fez.

Cleanliness was not the most marked characteristic of the conversation to which he lent a listless ear. It was no prurient curiosity that fixed his attention on this placid exchange of obscenities: he had lived too long in Morocco for obscenities not to have lost their savour. But he had never quite overcome the fascinated disgust with which he listened, nor the hope that one among the talkers would suddenly reveal some sense of a higher ideal, of what, at home, the earnest women he knew used solemnly to call a Purpose. He was sure that, some day, such a sign would come, and then--

Meanwhile, at that hour, there was nothing on earth to do in Eloued but to stand and listen--

The bazaar was beginning to fill up. Looking down the vaulted tunnel which led to the coffee-house the young man watched the thickening throng of shoppers and idlers. The fat merchant whose shop faced the end of the tunnel had just ridden up and rolled off his mule, while his black boy unbarred the door of the niche hung with embroidered slippers where the master throned. The young man in the faded caftan, watching the merchant scramble up and sink into his cushions, wondered for the thousandth time what he thought about all day in his dim stifling kennel, and what he did when he was away from it...for no length of residence in that dark land seemed to bring one nearer to finding out what the heathen thought and did when the eye of the Christian was off him.

Suddenly a wave of excitement ran through the crowd. Every head turned in the same direction, and even the camels bent their frowning faces and stretched their necks all one way, as animals do before a storm. A wild hoot had penetrated the bazaar, howling through the long white tunnels and under the reed-woven roofs like a Djinn among dishonoured graves. The heart of the young man began to beat.

"It sounds," he thought, "like a motor..."

But a motor at Eloued! There was one, every one knew, in the Sultan's Palace. It had been brought there years ago by a foreign Ambassador, as a gift from his sovereign, and was variously reported to be made entirely of aluminium, platinum or silver. But the parts had never been put together, the body had long been used for breeding silk-worms in--a not wholly successful experiment--and the acetylene lamps adorned the Pasha's gardens on state occasions. As for the horn, it had been sent as a gift, with a choice panoply of arms, to the Caïd of the Red Mountain; but as the india-rubber bulb had accidentally been left behind, it was certainly not the Caïd's visit which the present discordant cries announced...

"Hullo, you old dromedary! How's the folks up state?" cried a ringing voice. The awestruck populace gave way, and a young man in linen duster and motor cap, slipping under the interwoven necks of the astonished camels, strode down the tunnel with an air of authority and clapped a hand on the dreamer in the doorway.

"Harry Spink!" the latter gasped in a startled whisper, and with an intonation as un-African as his friend's. At the same instant he glanced over his shoulder, and his mild lips formed a cautious: "'sh."

"Who'd you take me for--Gabby Deslys?" asked the newcomer gaily; then, seeing that this topical allusion hung fire: "And what the dickens are you 'hushing' for, anyhow? You don't suppose, do you, that anybody in the bazaar thinks you're a *native*? D'y' ever look at your chin? Or that Adam's apple running up and down you like a bead on a billiard marker's wire? See here, Willard Bent..."

The young man in the caftan blushed distressfully, not so

much at the graphic reference to his looks as at the doubt cast on his disguise.

"I do assure you, Harry, I pick up a great deal of...of useful information...in this way..."

"Oh, get out," said Harry Spink cheerfully. "You believe all that still, do you? What's the good of it all, anyway?"

Willard Bent passed a hand under the other's arm and led him through the coffeehouse into an empty room at the back. They sat down on a shelf covered with matting and looked at each other earnestly.

"Don't *you* believe any longer, Harry Spink?" asked Willard Bent.

"Don't have to. I'm travelling for rubber now."

"Oh, merciful heaven! Was that your automobile?"

"Sure."

There was a long silence, during which

Bent sat with bowed head gazing on the earthen floor, while the bead in his throat performed its most active gymnastics. At last he lifted his eyes and fixed them on the tight red face of his companion.

"When did your faith fail you?" he asked.

The other considered him humorously. "Why--when I got onto this job, I guess."

Willard Bent rose and held out his hand.

"Good-bye...I must go...If I can be of any use...you know where to find me..."

"Any use? Say, old man, what's wrong? Are you trying to shake me?" Bent was silent, and Harry Spink continued insidiously: "Ain't you a mite hard on me? I thought the heathen was just what you was laying for."

Bent smiled mournfully. "There's no use trying to convert a renegade."

"That what I am? Well--all right. But how about the others? Say--let's order a lap of tea and have it out right here."

Bent seemed to hesitate; but at length he rose, put back the matting that screened the inner room, and said a word to the proprietor. Presently a scrofulous boy with gazelle eyes brought a brass tray bearing glasses and pipes of *kif*, gazed earnestly at the stranger in the linen duster, and slid back behind the matting.

"Of course," Bent began, "a good many people know I am a Baptist missionary"--("*No?*" from Spink, incredulously)--"but in the crowd of the bazaar they don't notice me, and I hear things..."

"Golly! I should suppose you did."

"I mean, things that may be useful. You know Mr. Blandhorn's idea..."

A tinge of respectful commiseration veiled the easy impudence of the drummer's look. "The old man still here, is he?"

"Oh, yes; of course. He will never leave Eloued."

"And the missus--?"

Bent again lowered his naturally low voice. "She died--a year ago--of the climate. The doctor had warned her; but Mr. Blandhorn felt a call to remain here."

"And she wouldn't leave without him?"

"Oh, *she* felt a call too...among the women..."

Spink pondered. "How many years you been here, Willard?"

"Ten next July," the other responded, as if he had added up the weeks and months so often that the reply was always on his lips.

"And the old man?"

"Twenty-five last April. We had planned a celebration... before Mrs. Blandhorn died. There was to have been a testimonial offered...but, owing to her death, Mr. Blandhorn preferred to devote the sum to our dispensary."

"I see. How much?" said Spink sharply.

"It wouldn't seem much to you. I believe about fifty pesetas...

"Two pesetas a year? Lucky the Society looks after you, ain't it?"

Willard Bent met his ironic glance steadily. "We're not here to trade," he said with dignity.

"No--that's right too--" Spink reddened slightly. "Well, all I meant was--look at here, Willard, we're old friends, even if I did go wrong, as I suppose you'd call it. I was in this thing near on a year myself, and what always tormented me was this: *What does it all amount to?*"

"Amount to?"

"Yes. I mean, what's the results? Supposing you was a fisherman. Well, if you fished a bit of river year after year, and never had a nibble, you'd do one of two things, wouldn't you? Move away--or lie about it. See?"

Bent nodded without speaking. Spink set down his glass and busied himself with the lighting of his long slender pipe. "Say, this mint-julep feels like old times," he remarked.

Bent continued to gaze frowningly into his untouched glass. At length he swallowed the sweet decoction at a gulp, and turned to his companion.

"I'd never lie..." he murmured. "Well--"

"I'm--I'm still--waiting..."

"Waiting--?"

"Yes. The wind bloweth where it listeth. If St. Paul had stopped to count...in Corinth, say. As I take it--" he looked long and passionately at the drummer--"as I take it, the thing is to *be* St. Paul."

Harry Spink remained unimpressed. "That's all talk--I heard all that when I was here before. What I want to know is: What's your bag? How many?"

"It's difficult--"

"I see: like the pigs. They run around so!"

Both the young men were silent, Spink pulling at his pipe, the other sitting with bent head, his eyes obstinately fixed on the beaten floor. At length Spink rose and tapped the missionary on the shoulder.

"Say--s'posin' we take a look around Corinth? I got to get onto my job tomorrow, but I'd like to take a turn round the old place first."

Willard Bent rose also. He felt singularly old and tired, and his mind was full of doubt as to what he ought to do. If he refused to accompany Harry Spink, a former friend and fellow-worker, it might look like running away from his questions...

They went out together.

CHAPTER II

The bazaar was seething. It seemed impossible that two more people should penetrate the throng of beggars, pilgrims, traders, slave-women, water-sellers, hawkers of dates and sweetmeats, leather-gaitered country-people carrying bunches of hens head-downward, jugglers' touts from the market-place, Jews in black caftans and greasy turbans, and scrofulous children reaching up to the high counters to fill their jars and baskets. But every now and then the Arab "Look out!" made the crowd divide and flatten itself against the stalls, and a long line of donkeys loaded with water-barrels or bundles of reeds, a string of musk-scented camels swaying their necks like horizontal question marks, or a great man perched on a pink-saddled mule and followed by slaves and clients, swept through the narrow passage without other peril to the pedestrians than that of a fresh exchange of vermin.

As the two young men drew back to make way for one of these processions, Willard Bent lifted his head and looked at his friend with a smile. "That's what Mr. Blandhorn says we ought to remember--it's one of his favourite images."

"What is?" asked Harry Spink, following with attentive gaze the movements of a young Jewess whose uncovered face and bright head-dress stood out against a group of muffled Arab women.

Instinctively Willard's voice took on a hortatory roll.

"Why, the way this dense mass of people, so heedless, so preoccupied, is imperceptibly penetrated--"

"By a handful of asses? That's so. But the asses have got some kick in 'em, remember!"

The missionary flushed to the edge of his fez, and his mild eyes grew dim. It was the old story: Harry Spink invariably got the better of him in bandying words--and the interpretation of allegories had never been his strong point. Mr. Blandhorn always managed to make them sound unanswerable, whereas on his disciple's lips they fell to pieces at a touch. What *was* it that Willard always left out?

A mournful sense of his unworthiness overcame him, and with it the discouraged vision of all the long months and years spent in the struggle with heat and dust and flies and filth and wickedness, the long lonely years of his youth that would never come back to him. It was the vision he most dreaded, and turning from it he tried to forget himself in watching his friend.

"Golly! The vacuum-cleaner ain't been round since my last visit," Mr. Spink observed, as they slipped in a mass of offal beneath a butcher's stall. "Let's get into another soukh--the flies here beat me."

They turned into another long lane chequered with a criss-cross of black reed-shadows. It was the saddlers' quarter, and here an even thicker crowd wriggled and swayed between the cramped stalls hung with bright leather and spangled ornaments.

"Say! It might be a good idea to import some of this stuff for Fourth of July processions--Knights of Pythias and Secret Societies' kinder thing," Spink mused, pausing before the brilliant spectacle. At the same moment a lad in an almond-green caftan sidled up and touched his arm.

Willard's face brightened. "Ah, that's little Ahmed--you don't remember him? Surely--the water-carrier's boy. Mrs. Blandhorn saved his mother's life when he was born, and he still comes to prayers. Yes, Ahmed, this is your old friend Mr. Spink."

Ahmed raised prodigious lashes from seraphic eyes and reverently surveyed the face of his old friend. "Me 'member."

"Hullo, old chap...why, of course...so do I," the drummer beamed. The missionary laid a brotherly hand on the boy's shoulder. It was really providential that Ahmed--whom they hadn't seen at the Mission for more weeks than Willard cared to count--should have "happened by" at that moment: Willard took it as a rebuke to his own doubts.

"You'll be in this evening for prayers, won't you, Ahmed?" he said, as if Ahmed never failed them. "Mr. Spink will be with us."

"Yessir," said Ahmed with unction. He slipped from under Willard's hand, and outflanking the drummer approached him from the farther side.

"Show you Souss boys dance? Down to old Jewess's, Bab-el-Soukh," he breathed angelically.

Willard saw his companion turn from red to a wrathful purple.

"Get out, you young swine, you--do you hear me?"

Ahmed grinned, wavered and vanished, engulfed in the careless crowd. The young men walked on without speaking.

CHAPTER III

In the market-place they parted. Willard Bent, after some hesitation, had asked Harry Spink to come to the Mission that evening. "You'd better come to supper--then we can talk quietly afterward. Mr. Blandhorn will want to see you," he suggested; and Mr. Spink had affably acquiesced.

The prayer-meeting was before supper, and Willard would have liked to propose that his friend should come to that also; but he did not dare. He said to himself that Harry Spink, who had been merely a lay assistant, might have lost the habit of reverence, and that it would be too painful to risk his scandalizing Mr. Blandhorn. But that was only a sham reason; and Willard, with his incorrigible habit of self-exploration, fished up the real one from a lower depth. What he had most feared was that there would be no one at the meeting.

During Mrs. Blandhorn's lifetime there had been no reason for such apprehension: they could always count on a few people. Mrs. Blandhorn, who had studied medicine at Ann Arbor, Michigan, had early gained renown in Eloued by her miraculous healing powers. The dispensary, in those days, had been beset by anxious-eyed women who unwound skinny fig-coloured children from their dirty draperies; and there had even been a time when Mr. Blandhorn had appealed to the Society for a young lady missionary to assist

119

his wife. But, for reasons not quite clear to Willard Bent, Mrs. Blandhorn, a thin-lipped determined little woman, had energetically opposed the coming of this youthful "Sister," and had declared that their Jewish maid-servant, old Myriem, could give her all the aid she needed.

Mr. Blandhorn yielded, as he usually did--as he had yielded, for instance, when one day, in a white inarticulate fury, his wife had banished her godson, little Ahmed (whose life she had saved), and issued orders that he should never show himself again except at prayer-meeting, and accompanied by his father. Mrs. Blandhorn, small, silent and passionate, had always--as Bent made out in his long retrospective musings--ended by having her way in the conflicts that occasionally shook the monotony of life at the Mission. After her death the young man had even suspected, beneath his superior's sincere and vehement sorrow, a lurking sense of relief. Mr. Blandhorn had snuffed the air of freedom, and had been, for the moment, slightly intoxicated by it. But not for long. Very soon his wife's loss made itself felt as a lasting void.

She had been (as Spink would have put it) "the whole show"; had led, inspired, organized her husband's work, held it together, and given it the brave front it presented to the unheeding heathen. Now the heathen had almost entirely fallen away, and the too evident inference was that they had come rather for Mrs. Blandhorn's pills than for her husband's preaching. Neither of the missionaries had avowed this discovery to the other, but to Willard at least it was implied in all the circumlocutions and evasions of their endless talks.

The young man's situation had been greatly changed by Mrs. Blandhorn's death. His superior had grown touchingly dependent on him. Their conversation, formerly confined to parochial matters, now ranged from abstruse doctrinal problems to the question of how to induce Myriem, who had deplorably "relapsed," to keep the kitchen cleaner and spend less time on the roofs. Bent felt that Mr. Blandhorn needed him at every moment, and that, during any prolonged absence, something vaguely "unfortunate" might happen at the Mission.

"I'm glad Spink has come; it will do him good to see somebody from outside," Willard thought, nervously hoping that Spink (a good fellow at bottom) would not trouble Mr. Blandhorn by any of his "unsettling" questions.

At the end of a labyrinth of lanes, on the farther side of the Jewish quarter, a wall of heat-cracked clay bore the inscription: "American Evangelical Mission." Underneath it a door opened into a court where an old woman in a bright head-dress sat under a fig-tree pounding something in a mortar.

She looked up, and, rising, touched Bent's draperies with her lips. Her small face, withered as a dry medlar, was full of an ancient wisdom: Mrs. Blandhorn had certainly been right in trusting Myriem.

A narrow house-front looked upon the court. Bent climbed the stairs to Mr. Blandhorn's study. It was a small room with a few dog-eared books on a set of rough shelves, the table at which Mr. Blandhorn wrote his reports for the Society, and a mattress covered with a bit of faded carpet, on which he slept. Near the window stood Mrs. Blandhorn's sewing-machine; it had never been moved since her death.

The missionary was sitting in the middle of the room, in the rocking chair which had also been his wife's. His large veined hands were clasped about its arms and his head rested against a patch-work cushion tied to the back by a shoe-lace. His mouth was slightly open, and a deep breath, occasionally rising to a whistle, proceeded with rhythmic regularity from his delicately-cut nostrils. Even surprised in sleep he was a fine man to look upon; and when, at the sound of Bent's approach, he opened his eyes and pulled himself out of his chair, he became magnificent. He had taken off his turban, and thrown a handkerchief over his head, which was shaved like an Arab's for coolness. His long beard was white, with the smoker's yellow tinge about the lips; but his eyebrows were jet-black, arched and restless. The gray eyes beneath them shed a mild benedictory beam, confirmed by the smile of a mouth which might have seemed weak if the beard had not so nearly concealed it. But the forehead menaced, fulminated or awed with the ever-varying play of the eyebrows. Willard

Bent never beheld that forehead without thinking of Sinai.

Mr. Blandhorn brushed some shreds of tobacco from his white djellabah and looked impressively at his assistant.

"The heat is really overwhelming," he said, as if excusing himself. He readjusted his turban, and then asked: "Is everything ready downstairs?"

Bent assented, and they went down to the long bare room where the prayer-meetings were held. In Mrs. Blandhorn's day it had also served as the dispensary, and a cupboard containing drugs and bandages stood against the wall under the text: "*Come unto me, all ye that labour and are heavy laden.*"

Myriem, abandoning her mortar, was vaguely tidying the Arab tracts and leaflets that lay on the divan against the wall. At one end of the room stood a table covered with a white cloth, with a Bible lying on it; and to the left a sort of pulpit-lectern, from which Mr. Blandhorn addressed his flock. In the doorway squatted Ayoub, a silent gray-headed negro; Bent, on his own arrival at Eloued, ten years earlier, had found him there in the same place and the same attitude. Ayoub was supposed to be a rescued slave from the Soudan, and was shown to visitors as "our first convert." He manifested no interest at the approach of the missionaries, but continued to gaze out into the sun-baked court cut in half by the shadow of the fig-tree.

Mr. Blandhorn, after looking about the empty room

as if he were surveying the upturned faces of an attentive congregation, placed himself at the lectern, put on his spectacles, and turned over the pages of his prayer-book. Then he knelt and bowed his head in prayer. His devotions ended, he rose and seated himself in the cane arm-chair that faced the lectern. Willard Bent sat opposite in another arm-chair. Mr. Blandhorn leaned back, breathing heavily, and passing his handkerchief over his face and brow. Now and then he drew out his watch, now and then he said: "The heat is really overwhelming."

Myriem had drifted back to her fig-tree, and the sound of the pestle mingled with the drone of flies on the window-pane. Occasionally the curses of a muleteer or the rhythmic chant of a water-carrier broke the silence; once there came from a neighbouring roof the noise of a short cat-like squabble ending in female howls; then the afternoon heat laid its leaden hush on all things.

Mr. Blandhorn opened his mouth and slept.

Willard Bent, watching him, thought with wonder and admiration of his past. What had he not seen, what secrets were not hidden in his bosom? By dint of sheer "sticking it out" he had acquired to the younger man a sort of visible sanctity. Twenty-five years of Eloued! He had known the old mad torturing Sultan, he had seen, after the defeat of the rebels, the long line of prisoners staggering in under a torrid sky, chained wrist to wrist, and dragging between them the putrefying bodies of those who had died on the march. He had seen the Great Massacre, when the rivers were red with French blood, and the Blandhorns had hidden an officer's wife and children in the rat-haunted drain under the court; he had known robbery and murder and intrigue, and all the dark maleficence of Africa; and he remained as serene, as confident and guileless, as on the day when he had first set foot on that evil soil, saying to himself (as he had told Willard): "*I will tread upon the lion and the adder, the young lion and the dragon will I tread under foot.*"

Willard Bent hated Africa; but it awed and fascinated him. And as he contemplated the splendid old man sleeping opposite him, so mysterious, so childlike and so weak (Mrs. Blandhorn had left him no doubts on that point), the disciple marvelled at the power of the faith which had armed his master with a sort of infantile strength against such dark and manifold perils.

Suddenly a shadow fell in the doorway, and Bent, roused from his dream, saw Harry Spink tiptoeing past the unmoved Ayoub. The drummer paused and looked with astonishment from one of the missionaries to the other. "Say," he asked, "is prayer-meeting over? I thought I'd be round in time."

He spoke seriously, even respectfully; it was plain that he felt flippancy to be out of place. But Bent suspected a lurking malice under his astonishment: he was sure Harry Spink had come to "count heads."

Mr. Blandhorn, wakened by the voice, stood up heavily.

"Harry Spink! Is it possible you are amongst us?"

"Why, yes, sir--I'm amongst. Didn't Willard tell you? I guess Willard Bent's ashamed of me."

Spink, with a laugh, shook Mr. Bland-horn's hand, and glanced about the empty room.

"I'm only here for a day or so--on business. Willard'll explain. But I wanted to come round to meeting--like old times. Sorry it's over."

The missionary looked at him with a grave candour. "It's not over--it has not begun. The overwhelming heat has probably kept away our little flock."

"I see," interpolated Spink.

"But now," continued Mr. Blandhorn with majesty, "that two or three are gathered together in His name, there is no reason why we should wait.--Myriem! Ayoub!"

He took his place behind the lectern and began: "Almighty and merciful Father--"

CHAPTER IV

The night was exceedingly close. Willard Bent, after Spink's departure, had undressed and stretched himself on his camp bed; but the mosquitoes roared like lions, and lying down made him more wakeful.

"In any Christian country," he mused, "this would mean a thunderstorm and a cool-off. Here it just means months and months more of the same thing." And he thought enviously of Spink, who, in two or three days, his "deal" concluded, would be at sea again, heading for the north.

Bent was honestly distressed at his own state of mind: he had feared that Harry Spink would "unsettle" Mr. Blandhorn, and, instead, it was he himself who had been unsettled. Old slumbering distrusts and doubts, bursting through his surface-apathy, had shot up under the drummer's ironic eye. It was not so much Spink, individually, who had loosened the crust of Bent's indifference; it was the fact of feeling his whole problem suddenly viewed and judged from the outside. At Eloued, he was aware, nobody, for a long time, had thought much about the missionaries. The French authorities were friendly, the Pacha was tolerant, the American Consul at Mogador had always stood by them in any small difficulties. But beyond that they were virtually non-existent. Nobody's view of life was really affected by their presence in the great swarming mysterious city: if they should pack up and leave that night, the story-tellers of the market would not interrupt their tales, or one less bargain be struck in the bazaar. Ayoub would still doze in the door, and old Myriem continue her secret life on the roofs...

The roofs were of course forbidden to the missionaries, as they are to men in all Moslem cities. But the Mission-house stood close to the walls, and Mr. Blandhorn's room, across the passage, gave on a small terrace overhanging the court of a caravansary upon which it was no sin to look. Willard wondered if it were any cooler on the terrace.

Some one tapped on his open door, and Mr. Blandhorn, in turban and caftan, entered the room, shading a small lamp.

"My dear Willard--can you sleep?"

"No, sir." The young man stumbled to his feet.

"Nor I. The heat is really...Shall we seek relief on the terrace?"

Bent followed him, and having extinguished the lamp Mr. Blandhorn led the way out. He dragged a strip of matting to the edge of the parapet, and the two men sat down on it side by side.

There was no moon, but a sky so full of stars that the city was outlined beneath it in great blue-gray masses. The air was motionless, but every now and then a wandering tremor stirred it and died out. Close under the parapet lay the bales and saddle-packs of the caravansary, between vaguer heaps, presumably of sleeping camels. In one corner, the star-glitter picked out the shape of a trough brimming with water, and stabbed it with long silver beams. Beyond the court rose the crenellations of the city walls, and above them one palm stood up like a tree of bronze.

"Africa--" sighed Mr. Blandhorn.

Willard Bent started at the secret echo of his own thoughts.

"Yes. Never anything else, sir--"

"Ah--" said the old man.

A tang-tang of stringed instruments, accompanied by the lowing of an earthenware drum, rose exasperatingly through the night. It was the kind of noise that, one knew, had been going on for hours before one began to notice it, and would go on, unchecked and unchanging, for endless hours more: like the heat, like the drought--like Africa.

Willard slapped at a mosquito.

"It's a party at the wool-merchant's, Myriem tells me," Mr. Blandhorn remarked. It really seemed as if, that night, the thoughts of the two men met without the need of words. Willard Bent was aware that, for both, the casual phrase had called up all the details of the scene: fat merchants in white bunches on their cushions, negresses coming and going with trays of sweets, champagne clandestinely poured, ugly singing-girls yowling, slim boys in petticoats dancing-- perhaps little Ahmed among them.

"I went down to the court just now. Ayoub has disappeared,"

129

Mr. Blandhorn continued. "Of course. When I heard in the bazaar that a black caravan was in from the south I knew he'd be off..."

Mr. Blandhorn lowered his voice. "Willard--have you reason to think...that Ayoub joins in their rites?"

"Myriem has always said he was a Hamatcha, sir. Look at those queer cuts and scars on him...It's a much bloodier sect than the Aissaouas."

Through the nagging throb of the instruments came a sound of human wailing, cadenced, terrible, relentless, carried from a long way off on a lift of the air. Then the air died, and the wailing with it.

"From somewhere near the Potter's Field...there's where the caravan is camping," Willard murmured.

The old man made no answer. He sat with his head bowed, his veined hands grasping his knees; he seemed to his disciple to be whispering fragments of Scripture.

"Willard, my son, this is our fault," he said at length.

"What--? Ayoub?"

"Ayoub is a poor ignorant creature, hardly more than an animal. Even when he witnessed for Jesus I was not very sure the Word reached him. I refer to--to what Harry Spink said this evening...It has kept me from sleeping, Willard Bent."

"Yes--I know, sir."

"Harry Spink is a worldly-minded man. But he is not a bad man. He did a manly thing when he left us, since he did not feel the call. But we have felt the call, Willard, you and I--and when a man like Spink puts us a question such as he put this evening we ought to be able to answer it. And we ought not to want to avoid answering it."

"You mean when he said: '*What is there in it for Jesus?*'"

"The phrase was irreverent, but the meaning reached me. He meant, I take it: 'What have your long years here profited to Christ?' You understood it so--?"

"Yes. He said to me in the bazaar: 'What's your bag?'"

Mr. Blandhorn sighed heavily. For a few minutes Willard fancied he had fallen asleep; but he lifted his head and, stretching his hand out, laid it on his disciple's arm.

"The Lord chooses His messengers as it pleaseth Him: I have been awaiting this for a long time." The young man felt his arm strongly grasped. "Willard, you have been much to me all these years; but that is nothing. All that matters is what you are to Christ...and the test of that, at this moment, is your willingness to tell me the exact truth, as you see it."

Willard Bent felt as if he were a very tall building, and his heart a lift suddenly dropping down from the roof to the cellar. He stirred nervously, releasing his arm, and cleared his throat; but he made no answer. Mr. Blandhorn went on.

"Willard, this is the day of our accounting--of *my* accounting. What have I done with my twenty-five years in Africa? I might deceive myself as long as my wife lived--I cannot now." He added, after a pause: "Thank heaven *she* never doubted..."

The younger man, with an inward shiver, remembered some of Mrs. Blandhorn's confidences. "I suppose that's what marriage is," he mused--"just a fog, like everything else."

Aloud he asked: "Then why should you doubt, sir?"

"Because my eyes have been opened--"

"By Harry Spink?" the disciple sneered.

The old man raised his hand. "'*Out of the mouths of babes--*' But it is not Harry Spink who first set me thinking. He has merely loosened my tongue. He has been the humble instrument compelling me to exact the truth of you."

Again Bent felt his heart dropping down a long dark shaft. He found no words at the bottom of it, and Mr. Blandhorn continued: "The truth and the whole truth, Willard Bent. We have failed--*I* have failed. We have not reached the souls of these people. Those who still come to us do so from interested motives--or, even if I do some few of them an injustice, if there is in some a blind yearning for the light, is there one among them whose eyes we have really opened?"

Willard Bent sat silent, looking up and down the long years, as if to summon from the depths of memory some single incident that should permit him to say there was.

"You don't answer, my poor young friend. Perhaps you have been clearer-sighted; perhaps you saw long ago that we were not worthy of our hire."

"I never thought that of you, sir!"

"Nor of yourself? For we have been one--or so I have believed--in all our hopes and efforts. Have you been satisfied with *your* results?"

Willard saw the dialectical trap, but some roused force in him refused to evade it. "No, sir--God knows."

"Then I am answered. We have failed: Africa has beaten us. It has always been my way, as you know, Willard, to face the truth squarely," added the old man who had lived so long in dreams; "and now that *this* truth has been borne in on me, painful as it is, I must act on it...act in accordance with its discovery."

He drew a long breath, as if oppressed by the weight of his resolution, and sat silent for a moment, fanning his face with a corner of his white draperies.

"And here too--here too I must have your help, Willard," he began presently, his hand again weighing on the young man's arm. "I will tell you the conclusions I have reached; and you must answer me--as you would answer your Maker."

"Yes, sir."

The old man lowered his voice. "It is our lukewarmness, Willard--it is nothing else. We have not witnessed for Christ as His saints and martyrs witnessed for Him. What have we done to fix the attention of these people, to convince them of our zeal, to overwhelm them with the irresistibleness of the Truth? Answer me on your word--what have we done?"

Willard pondered. "But the saints and martyrs...were

persecuted, sir."

"*Persecuted!* You have spoken the word I wanted."

"But the people here," Willard argued, "don't *want* to persecute anybody. They're not fanatical unless you insult their religion."

Mr. Blandhorn's grasp grew tighter. "Insult their religion! That's it...tonight you find just the words..."

Willard felt his arm shake with the tremor that passed through the other's body. "The saints and martyrs insulted the religion of the heathen--they spat on it, Willard--they rushed into the temples and knocked down the idols. They said to the heathen: 'Turn away your faces from all your abominations'; and after the manner of men they fought with beasts at Ephesus. What is the Church on earth called? The Church Militant! You and I are soldiers of the Cross."

The missionary had risen and stood leaning against the parapet, his right arm lifted as if he spoke from a pulpit. The music at the wool-merchant's had ceased, but now and then, through the midnight silence, there came an echo of ritual howls from the Potters' Field.

Willard was still seated, his head thrown back against the parapet, his eyes raised to Mr. Blandhorn. Following the gesture of the missionary's lifted hand, from which the muslin fell back like the sleeve of a surplice, the young man's gaze was led upward to another white figure, hovering small and remote above their heads. It was a muezzin leaning from his airy balcony to drop on the blue-gray masses of the starlit city the cry: "Only Allah is great."

Mr. Blandhorn saw the white figure too, and stood facing it with motionless raised arm.

"Only Christ is great, only Christ crucified!" he suddenly shouted in Arabic with all the strength of his broad lungs.

The figure paused, and seemed to Willard to bend over, as if peering down in their direction; but a moment later it had moved to the other corner of the balcony, and the cry fell again on the sleeping roofs:

"Allah--Allah--only Allah!"

"Christ--Christ--only Christ crucified!" roared Mr. Blandhorn, exalted with wrath and shaking his fist at the aerial puppet.

The puppet once more paused and peered; then it moved on and vanished behind the flank of the minaret.

The missionary, still towering with lifted arm, dusky-faced in the starlight, seemed to Willard to have grown in majesty and stature. But presently his arm fell and his head sank into his hands. The young man knelt down, hiding his face also, and they prayed in silence, side by side, while from the farther corners of the minaret, less audibly, fell the infidel call.

Willard, his prayer ended, looked up, and saw that the old man's garments were stirred as if by a ripple of air. But the air was quite still, and the disciple perceived that the tremor of the muslin was communicated to it by Mr. Blandhorn's body.

"He's trembling--trembling all over. He's afraid of something. What's he afraid of?" And in the same breath Willard had answered his own question: "He's afraid of what he's made up his mind to do."

CHAPTER V

Two days later Willard Bent sat in the shade of a ruined tomb outside the Gate of the Graves, and watched the people streaming in to Eloued. It was the eve of the feast of the local saint, Sidi Oman, who slept in a corner of the Great Mosque, under a segment of green-tiled cupola, and was held in deep reverence by the country people, many of whom belonged to the powerful fraternity founded in his name.

The ruin stood on a hillock beyond the outer wall. From where the missionary sat he overlooked the fortified gate and the irregular expanse of the Potters' Field, with its primitive furnaces built into hollows of the ground, between ridges shaded by stunted olive-trees. On the farther side of the trail which the pilgrims followed on entering the gate lay a sun-blistered expanse dotted with crooked grave-stones, where hucksters traded, and the humblest caravans camped in a waste of refuse, offal and stripped date-branches. A cloud of dust, perpetually subsiding and gathering again, hid these sordid details from Bent's eyes, but not from his imagination.

"Nowhere in Eloued," he thought with a shudder, "are the flies as fat and blue as they are inside that gate."

But this was a fugitive reflection: his mind was wholly absorbed in what had happened in the last forty-eight hours, and what was likely to happen in the next.

"To think," he mused, "that after ten years I don't really know him...A labourer in the Lord's vineyard--shows how much good I am!"

His thoughts were moody and oppressed with fear. Never, since his first meeting with Mr. Blandhorn, had he pondered so deeply the problem of his superior's character. He tried to deduce from the past some inference as to what Mr. Blandhorn was likely to do next; but, as far as he knew, there was nothing in the old man's previous history resembling the midnight scene on the Mission terrace.

That scene had already had its repercussion.

On the following morning, Willard, drifting as usual about the bazaar, had met a friendly French official, who, taking him aside, had told him there were strange reports abroad-- which he hoped Mr. Bent would be able to deny...In short, as it had never been Mr. Blandhorn's policy to offend the native population, or insult their religion, the Administration was confident that...

Surprised by Willard's silence, and visibly annoyed at being obliged to pursue the subject, the friendly official, growing graver, had then asked what had really occurred; and, on Willard's replying, had charged him with an earnest recommendation to his superior--a warning, if necessary-- that the government would not, under any circumstances, tolerate a repetition..."But I daresay it was the heat?" he concluded; and Willard weakly acquiesced.

He was ashamed now of having done so; yet, after all, how did he know it was not the heat? A heavy sanguine man like Mr. Blandhorn would probably never quite accustom himself to the long strain of the African summer. "Or his wife's death--" he had murmured to the sympathetic official, who smiled with relief at the suggestion.

And now he sat overlooking the enigmatic city, and asking himself again what he really knew of his superior. Mr. Blandhorn had come to Eloued as a young man, extremely poor, and dependent on the pittance which the Missionary Society at that time gave to its representatives. To ingratiate himself among the people (the expression was his own), and also to earn a few pesetas, he had worked as a carpenter in the bazaar, first in the soukh of the ploughshares and then in that of the cabinet-makers. His skill in carpentry had not been great, for his large eloquent hands were meant to wave from a pulpit, and not to use the adze or the chisel; but he had picked up a little Arabic (Willard always marvelled that it remained so little), and had made many acquaintances--and, as he thought, some converts. At any rate, no one, either then or later, appeared to wish him ill, and during the massacre his house had been respected, and the insurgents had even winked at the aid he had courageously given to the French.

Yes--he had certainly been courageous. There was in him, in spite of his weaknesses and his vacillations, a streak of moral heroism that perhaps only waited its hour...But hitherto his principle had always been that the missionary must win converts by kindness, by tolerance, and by the example of a blameless life.

Could it really be Harry Spink's question that had shaken him in this belief? Or was it the long-accumulated sense of inefficiency that so often weighed on his disciple? Or was it simply the call--did it just mean that their hour had come?

Shivering a little in spite of the heat, Willard pulled himself together and descended into the city. He had been seized with a sudden desire to know what Mr. Blandhorn was about, and avoiding the crowd he hurried back by circuitous lanes to the Mission. On the way he paused at a certain corner and looked into a court full of the murmur of water. Beyond it was an arcade detached against depths of shadow, in which a few lights glimmered. White figures, all facing one way, crouched and touched their foreheads to the tiles, the soles of their bare feet, wet with recent ablutions, turning up as their bodies swayed forward. Willard caught the scowl of a beggar on the threshold, and hurried past the forbidden scene.

He found Mr. Blandhorn in the meeting-room, tying up Ayoub's head.

"I do it awkwardly," the missionary mumbled, a safety-pin between his teeth. "Alas, my hands are not *hers*."

"What's he done to himself?" Willard growled; and above

the bandaged head Mr. Blandhorn's expressive eyebrows answered.

There was a dark stain on the back of Ayoub's faded shirt, and another on the blue scarf he wore about his head.

"Ugh--it's like cats slinking back after a gutter-fight," the young man muttered.

Ayoub wound his scarf over the bandages, shambled back to the doorway, and squatted down to watch the fig-tree.

The missionaries looked at each other across the empty room.

"What's the use, sir?" was on Willard's lips; but instead of speaking he threw himself down on the divan. There was to be no prayer-meeting that afternoon, and the two men sat silent, gazing at the back of Ayoub's head. A smell of disinfectants hung in the heavy air...

"Where's Myriem?" Willard asked, to say something.

"I believe she had a ceremony of some sort...a family affair..."

"A circumcision, I suppose?"

Mr. Blandhorn did not answer, and Willard was sorry he had made the suggestion. It would simply serve as another reminder of their failure...

He stole a furtive glance at Mr. Bland-horn, nervously wondering if the time had come to speak of the French official's warning. He had put off doing so, half-hoping it would not be necessary. The old man seemed so calm, so like

141

his usual self, that it might be wiser to let the matter drop. Perhaps he had already forgotten the scene on the terrace; or perhaps he thought he had sufficiently witnessed for the Lord in shouting his insult to the muezzin. But Willard did not really believe this: he remembered the tremor which had shaken Mr. Blandhorn after the challenge, and he felt sure it was not a retrospective fear.

"Our friend Spink has been with me," said Mr. Blandhorn suddenly. "He came in soon after you left."

"Ah? I'm sorry I missed him. I thought he'd gone, from his not coming in yesterday."

"No; he leaves tomorrow morning for Mogador." Mr Blandhorn paused, still absently staring at the back of Ayoub's neck; then he added: "I have asked him to take you with him."

"To take me--Harry Spink? In his automobile?" Willard gasped. His heart began to beat excitedly.

"Yes. You'll enjoy the ride. It's a long time since you've been away, and you're looking a little pulled down."

"You're very kind, sir: so is Harry." He paused. "But I'd rather not."

Mr. Blandhorn, turning slightly, examined him between half-dropped lids.

"I have business for you--with the Consul," he said with a certain sternness. "I don't suppose you will object--"

"Oh, of course not." There was another pause. "Could you

tell me--give me an idea--of what the business is, sir?"

It was Mr. Blandhorn's turn to appear perturbed. He coughed, passed his hand once or twice over his beard, and again fixed his gaze on Ayoub's inscrutable nape.

"I wish to send a letter to the Consul."

"A letter? If it's only a letter, couldn't Spink take it?"

"Undoubtedly. I might also send it by post--if I cared to transmit it in that manner. I presumed," added Mr. Blandhorn with threatening brows, "that you would understand I had my reasons--"

"Oh, in that case, of course, sir--" Willard hesitated, and then spoke with a rush. "I saw Lieutenant Lourdenay in the bazaar yesterday--" he began.

When he had finished his tale Mr. Bland-horn meditated for a long time in silence. At length he spoke in a calm voice. "And what did you answer, Willard?"

"I--I said I'd tell you--"

"Nothing more?"

"No. Nothing."

"Very well. We'll talk of all this more fully...when you get back from Mogador. Remember that Mr. Spink will be here before sunrise. I advised him to get away as early as possible on account of the Feast of Sidi Oman. It's always a poor day for foreigners to be seen about the streets."

CHAPTER VI

At a quarter before four on the morning of the Feast of Sidi Oman, Willard Bent stood waiting at the door of the Mission.

He had taken leave of Mr. Blandhorn the previous night, and stumbled down the dark stairs on bare feet, his bundle under his arm, just as the sky began to whiten around the morning star.

The air was full of a mocking coolness which the first ray of the sun would burn up; and a hush as deceptive lay on the city that was so soon to blaze with religious frenzy. Ayoub lay curled up on his doorstep like a dog, and old Myriem, presumably, was still stretched on her mattress on the roof.

What a day for a flight across the desert in Harry's tough little car! And after the hours of heat and dust and glare, how good, at twilight, to see the cool welter of the Atlantic, a spent sun dropping into it, and the rush of the stars...Dizzy with the vision, Willard leaned against the door-post with closed eyes.

A subdued hoot aroused him, and he hurried out to the car, which was quivering and growling at the nearest corner. The drummer nodded a welcome, and they began to wind cautiously between sleeping animals and huddled heaps of humanity till they reached the nearest gate.

On the waste land beyond the walls the people of the

caravans were already stirring, and pilgrims from the hills streaming across the palmetto scrub under emblazoned banners. As the sun rose the air took on a bright transparency in which distant objects became unnaturally near and vivid, like pebbles seen through clear water: a little turban-shaped tomb far off in the waste looked as lustrous as ivory, and a tiled minaret in an angle of the walls seemed to be carved out of turquoise. How Eloued lied to eyes looking back on it at sunrise!

"Something wrong," said Harry Spink, putting on the brake and stopping in the thin shade of a cork-tree. They got out and Willard leaned against the tree and gazed at the red walls of Eloued. They were already about two miles from the town, and all around them was the wilderness. Spink shoved his head into the bonnet, screwed and greased and hammered, and finally wiped his hands on a black rag and called out: "I thought so--. Jump in!"

Willard did not move.

"Hurry up, old man. She's all right, I tell you. It was just the carburettor."

The missionary fumbled under his draperies and pulled out Mr. Blandhorn's letter.

"Will you see that the Consul gets this tomorrow?"

"Will I--what the hell's the matter, Willard?" Spink dropped his rag and stared.

"I'm not coming. I never meant to."

145

The young men exchanged a long look.

"It's no time to leave Mr. Blandhorn--a day like this," Willard continued, moistening his dry lips.

Spink shrugged, and sounded a faint whistle. "Queer--!"

"What's queer?"

"He said just the same thing to me about *you*--wanted to get you out of Eloued on account of the goings on today. He said you'd been rather worked up lately about religious matters, and might do something rash that would get you both into trouble."

"Ah--" Willard murmured.

"And I believe you might, you know--you look sorter funny." Willard laughed.

"Oh, come along," his friend urged, disappointed.

"I'm sorry--I can't. I had to come this far so that he wouldn't know. But now I've got to go back. Of course what he told you was just a joke--but I must be there today to see that nobody bothers him."

Spink scanned his companion's face with friendly flippant eyes. "Well, I give up--. What's the *use*, when he don't want you?--Say," he broke off, "what's the truth of that story about the old man's having insulted a marabout in a mosque night before last? It was all over the bazaar--"

Willard felt himself turn pale. "Not a marabout. It was--where did you hear it?" he stammered.

"All over--the way you hear stories in these places."

"Well--it's not true." Willard lifted his bundle from the motor and tucked it under his arm. "I'm sorry, Harry--I've got to go back," he repeated.

"What? The Call, eh?" The sneer died on Spink's lips, and he held out his hand. "Well, I'm sorry too. So long." He turned the crank, scrambled into his seat, and cried back over his shoulder: "What's the *use*, when he don't want you?"

Willard was already labouring home across the plain.

After struggling along for half an hour in the sand he crawled under the shade of an abandoned well and sat down to ponder. Two courses were open to him, and he had not yet been able to decide between them. His first impulse was to go straight to the Mission, and present himself to Mr. Bland-horn. He felt sure, from what Spink had told him, that the old missionary had sent him away purposely, and the fact seemed to confirm his apprehensions. If Mr. Bland-horn wanted him away, it was not through any fear of his imprudence, but to be free from his restraining influence. But what act did the old man contemplate, in which he feared to involve his disciple? And if he were really resolved on some rash measure, might not Willard's unauthorized return merely serve to exasperate this resolve, and hasten whatever action he had planned?

The other step the young man had in mind was to go secretly to the French Administration, and there drop a hint of what he feared. It was the course his sober judgment commended. The echo of Spink's "What's the use?" was in his ears: it was the expression of his own secret doubt. What *was* the use? If dying could bring any of these darkened souls to the light...well, that would have been different. But what least sign was there that it would do anything but rouse their sleeping blood-lust?

Willard was oppressed by the thought that had always lurked beneath his other doubts. They talked, he and Mr. Blandhorn, of the poor ignorant heathen--but were not they themselves equally ignorant in everything that concerned the heathen? What did they know of these people, of their antecedents, the origin of their beliefs and superstitions, the meaning of their habits and passions and precautions? Mr. Blandhorn seemed never to have been troubled by this question, but it had weighed on Willard ever since he had come across a quiet French ethnologist who was studying the tribes of the Middle Atlas. Two or three talks with this traveller--or listenings to him--had shown Willard the extent of his own ignorance. He would have liked to borrow books, to read, to study; but he knew little French and no German, and he felt confusedly that there was in him no soil sufficiently prepared for facts so overwhelmingly new to root in it...And the heat lay on him, and the little semblance of his missionary duties deluded him...and he drifted...

As for Mr. Blandhorn, he never read anything but

the Scriptures, a volume of his own sermons (printed by subscription, to commemorate his departure for Morocco), and--occasionally--a back number of the missionary journal that arrived at Eloued at long intervals, in thick mouldy batches, Consequently no doubts disturbed him, and Willard felt the hopelessness of grappling with an ignorance so much deeper and denser than his own. Whichever way his mind turned, it seemed to bring up against the blank wall of Harry Spink's; "What's the use?"

He slipped through the crowds in the congested gateway, and made straight for the Mission. He had decided to go to the French Administration, but he wanted first to find out from the servants what Mr. Blandhorn was doing, and what his state of mind appeared to be.

The Mission door was locked, but Willard was not surprised; he knew the precaution was sometimes taken on feast days, though seldom so early. He rang, and waited impatiently for Myriem's old face in the crack; but no one came, and below his breath he cursed her with expurgated curses.

"Ayoub--*Ayoub!*" he cried, rattling at the door; but still no answer. Ayoub, apparently, was off too. Willard rang the bell again, giving the three long pulls of the "emergency call"; it was the summons which always roused Mr. Blandhorn. But no one came.

Willard shook and pounded, and hung on the bell till it

tinkled its life out in a squeak...but all in vain. The house was empty: Mr. Blandhorn was evidently out with the others.

Disconcerted, the young man turned, and plunged into the red clay purlieus behind the Mission. He entered a mud-hut where an emaciated dog, dozing on the threshold, lifted a recognizing lid, and let him by. It was the house of Ahmed's father, the water-carrier, and Willard knew it would be empty at that hour.

A few minutes later there emerged into the crowded streets a young American dressed in a black coat of vaguely clerical cut, with a soft felt hat shading his flushed cheek-bones, and a bead running up and down his nervous throat.

The bazaar was already full of a deep holiday rumour, like the rattle of wind in the palm-tops. The young man in the clerical coat, sharply examined as he passed by hundreds of long Arab eyes, slipped into the lanes behind the soukhs, and by circuitous passages gained the neighbourhood of the Great Mosque. His heart was hammering against his black coat, and under the buzz in his brain there boomed out insistently the old question: "What's the use?"

Suddenly, near the fountain that faced one of the doors of the Great Mosque, he saw the figure of a man dressed like himself. The eyes of the two men met across the crowd, and Willard pushed his way to Mr. Blandhorn's side.

"Sir, why did you--why are you--? I'm back--I couldn't help it," he gasped out disconnectedly.

He had expected a vehement rebuke; but the old missionary only smiled on him sadly. "It was noble of you, Willard...I understand..." He looked at the young man's coat. "We had the same thought--again--at the same hour." He paused, and drew Willard into the empty passage of a ruined building behind the fountain. "But what's the use,--what's the use?" he exclaimed.

The blood rushed to the young man's forehead. "Ah--then you feel it too?"

Mr. Blandhorn continued, grasping his arm: "I've been out--in this dress--ever since you left; I've hung about the doors of the Medersas, I've walked up to the very threshold of the Mosque, I've leaned against the wall of Sidi Oman's shrine; once the police warned me, and I pretended to go away...but I came back...I pushed up closer...I stood in the doorway of the Mosque, and they saw me...the people inside saw me...and no one touched me...I'm too harmless...*they don't believe in me!*"

He broke off, and under his struggling eyebrows Willard saw the tears on his old lids.

The young man gathered courage. "But don't you see, sir, that that's the reason it's no use? We don't understand them any more than they do us; they know it, and all our witnessing for Christ will make no difference."

Mr. Blandhorn looked at him sternly. "Young man, no Christian has the right to say that."

Willard ignored the rebuke. "Come home, sir, come home...it's no use..."

"It was because I foresaw you would take this view that I sent you to Mogador. Since I was right," exclaimed Mr. Blandhorn, facing round on him fiercely, "how is it you have disobeyed me and come back?"

Willard was looking at him with new eyes. All his majesty seemed to have fallen from him with his Arab draperies. How short and heavy and weak he looked in his scant European clothes! The coat, tightly strained across the stomach, hung above it in loose wrinkles, and the ill-fitting trousers revealed their wearer's impressive legs as slightly bowed at the knees. This diminution in his physical prestige was strangely moving to his disciple. What was there left, with that gone--?

"Oh, do come home, sir," the young man groaned. "Of course they don't care what we do--of course--"

"Ah--" cried Mr. Blandhorn, suddenly dashing past him into the open.

The rumour of the crowd had become a sort of roaring chant. Over the thousands of bobbing heads that packed every cranny of the streets leading to the space before the Mosque there ran the mysterious sense of something new, invisible, but already imminent. Then, with the strange Oriental elasticity, the immense throng divided, and a new throng poured through it, headed by riders ritually draped, and overhung with banners which seemed to be lifted and floated aloft on the shouts of innumerable throats. It was the Pasha of Eloued coming to pray at the tomb of Sidi Oman.

Into this mass Mr. Blandhorn plunged and disappeared, while Willard Bent, for an endless minute, hung back in the shelter of the passage, the old "What's the use?" in his ears.

A hand touched his sleeve, and a cracked voice echoed the words.

"What's the use, master?" It was old Myriem, clutching him with scared face and pulling out a limp djellabah from under her holiday shawl.

"I saw you...Ahmed's father told me..." (How everything was known in the bazaars!) "Here, put this on quick, and slip away. They won't trouble you..."

"Oh, but they will--they *shall!*" roared Willard, in a voice unknown to his own ears, as he flung off the old woman's hand and, trampling on the djellabah in his flight, dashed into the crowd at the spot where it had swallowed up his master.

They would--they *should!* No more doubting and weighing and conjecturing! The sight of the weak unwieldy old man, so ignorant, so defenceless and so convinced, disappearing alone into that red furnace of fanaticism, swept from the disciple's mind every thought but the single passion of devotion.

That he lay down his life for his friend--If he couldn't bring himself to believe in any other reason for what he was doing, that one seemed suddenly to be enough...

The crowd let him through, still apparently indifferent to his advance. Closer, closer he pushed to the doors of the Mosque, struggling and elbowing through a mass of people so densely jammed that the heat of their breathing was in his face, the rank taste of their bodies on his parched lips--closer, closer, till a last effort of his own thin body, which seemed a mere cage of ribs with a wild heart dashing against it, brought him to the doorway of the Mosque, where Mr. Blandhorn, his head thrown back, his arms crossed on his chest, stood steadily facing the heathen multitude.

As Willard reached his side their glances met, and the old man, glaring out under prophetic brows, whispered without moving his lips: "Now--*now!*"

Willard took it as a signal to follow, he knew not where or why: at that moment he had no wish to know.

Mr. Blandhorn, without waiting for an answer, had turned, and, doubling on himself, sprung into the great court of the Mosque. Willard breathlessly followed, the glitter of tiles and the blinding sparkle of fountains in his dazzled eyes...

The court was almost empty, the few who had been praying having shortened their devotions and joined the Pasha's train, which was skirting the outer walls of the Mosque to reach the shrine of Sidi Oman. Willard was conscious of a moment of detached reconnoitring: once or twice, from the roof of a deserted college to which the government architect had taken him, he had looked down furtively on the forbidden scene, and his sense of direction told him that the black figure speeding across the blazing mirror of wet tiles was making for the hall where the Koran was expounded to students.

Even now, as he followed, through the impending sense of something dangerous and tremendous he had the feeling that after all perhaps no one would bother them, that all the effort of will pumped up by his storming heart to his lucid brain might conceivably end in some pitiful anti-climax in the French Administration offices.

"They'll treat us like whipped puppies--"

But Mr. Blandhorn had reached the school, had disappeared under its shadowy arcade, and emerged again into the blaze of sunlight, clutching a great parchment Koran.

"Ah," thought Willard, "*now--!*"

He found himself standing at the missionary's side, so close that they must have made one black blot against the white-hot quiver of tiles. Mr. Blandhorn lifted up the Book and spoke.

"The God whom ye ignorantly worship, Him declare I unto you," he cried in halting Arabic.

A deep murmur came from the turbaned figures gathered under the arcade of the Mosque. Swarthy faces lowered, eyes gleamed like agate, teeth blazed under snarling lips; but the group stood motionless, holding back, visibly restrained by the menace of the long arm of the Administration.

"Him declare I unto you--Christ crucified!" cried Mr. Blandhorn.

An old man, detaching himself from the group, advanced across the tiles and laid his hand on the missionary's arm. Willard recognized the Cadi of the Mosque.

"You must restore the Book," the Cadi said gravely to Mr. Blandhorn, "and leave this court immediately; if not--"

He held out his hand to take the Koran. Mr. Blandhorn, in a flash, dodged the restraining arm, and, with a strange new elasticity of his cumbrous body, rolling and bouncing across the court between the dazed spectators, gained the gateway opening on the market-place behind the Mosque. The centre of the great dusty space was at the moment almost deserted. Mr. Blandhorn sprang forward, the Koran clutched to him, Willard panting at his heels, and the turbaned crowd after them, menacing but still visibly restrained.

In the middle of the square Mr. Bland-horn halted, faced about and lifted the Koran high above his head. Willard, rigid at his side, was obliquely conscious of the gesture, and at the same time aware that the free space about them was rapidly diminishing under the mounting tide of people swarming in from every quarter. The faces closest were no longer the gravely wrathful countenances of the Mosque, but lean fanatical masks of pilgrims, beggars, wandering "saints" and miracle-makers, and dark tribesmen of the hills careless of their creed but hot to join in the halloo against the hated stranger. Far off in the throng, bobbing like a float on the fierce sea of turbans, Willard saw the round brown face of a native officer frantically fighting his way through. Now and then the face bobbed nearer, and now and then a tug of the tide rolled it back.

Willard felt Mr. Blandhorn's touch on his arm.

"You're with me--?"

"Yes--"

The old man's voice sank and broke. "Say a word to... strengthen me...I can't find any...Willard," he whispered.

Willard's brain was a blank. But against the blank a phrase suddenly flashed out in letters of fire, and he turned and spoke it to his master. "*Say among the heathen that the Lord reigneth.*"

"Ah---." Mr. Blandhorn, with a gasp, drew himself to his full height and hurled the Koran down at his feet in the dung-strown dust.

"Him, Him declare I unto you--Christ crucified!" he thundered: and to Willard, in a fierce aside: "Now spit!"

Dazed a moment, the young man stood uncertain; then he saw the old missionary draw back a step, bend forward, and deliberately spit upon the sacred pages.

"This...is abominable..." the disciple thought; and, sucking up the last drop of saliva from his dry throat, he also bent and spat.

"Now trample--*trample!*" commanded Mr. Blandhorn,

his arms stretched out, towering black and immense, as if crucified against the flaming sky; and his foot came down on the polluted Book.

Willard, seized with the communicative frenzy, fell on his knees, tearing at the pages, and scattering them about him, smirched and defiled in the dust.

"Spit--spit! Trample--trample!...Christ! I see the heavens opened!" shrieked the old missionary, covering his eyes with his hands. But what he said next was lost to his disciple in the rising roar of the mob which had closed in on them. Far off, Willard caught a glimpse of the native officer's bobbing head, and then of Lieutenant Lourdenay's scared face. But a moment later he had veiled his own face from the sight of the struggle at his side. Mr. Blandhorn had fallen on his knees, and Willard heard him cry out once: "Sadie--*Sadie!*" It was Mrs. Blandhorn's name.

Then the young man was himself borne down, and darkness descended on him. Through it he felt the sting of separate pangs indescribable, melting at last into a general mist of pain. He remembered Stephen, and thought: "Now they're stoning me--" and tried to struggle up and reach out to Mr. Blandhorn...

But the market-place seemed suddenly empty, as though the throng of their assailants had been demons of the desert, the thin spirits of evil that dance on the noonday heat. Now the dusk seemed to have dispersed them, and Willard looked up and saw a quiet star above a wall, and heard the cry of the muezzin dropping down from a near-by minaret: "Allah-- Allah--only Allah is great!"

Willard closed his eyes, and in his great weakness felt the tears run down between his lids. A hand wiped them away, and he looked again, and saw the face of Harry Spink stooping over him.

He supposed it was a dream-Spink, and smiled a little, and the dream smiled back.

"Where am I?" Willard wondered to himself; and the dream-Spink answered: "In the hospital, you infernal fool. I got back too late--"

"You came back--?"

"Of course. Lucky I did--I I saw this morning you were off your base."

Willard, for a long time, lay still. Impressions reached him slowly, and he had to deal with them one by one, like a puzzled child.

At length he said: "Mr. Blandhorn--?" Spink bent his head, and his voice was grave in the twilight.

"They did for him in no time; I guess his heart was weak. I don't think he suffered. Anyhow, if he did he wasn't sorry; I know, because I saw his face before they buried him... Now you lie still, and I'll get you out of this tomorrow," he commanded, waving a fly-cloth above Willard's sunken head.

THE TEMPERATE ZONE

CHAPTER I

"Travelling, sir," a curt parlour-maid announced from Mrs. Donald Paul's threshold in Kensington; adding, as young Willis French's glance slipped over her shoulder down a narrow and somewhat conventional perspective of white panelling and black prints: "If there's any message you'd like to write"--

He did not know if there were or not; but he instantly saw that his hesitation would hold the house-door open a minute longer, and thus give him more time to stamp on his memory the details of the cramped London hall, beyond which there seemed no present hope of penetrating.

"Could you tell me where?" he asked, in a tone implying that the question of his having something to write might be determined by the nature of the answer.

The parlour-maid scrutinized him more carefully. "Not exactly, sir: Mr. and Mrs. Paul are away motoring, and I believe they're to cross over to the continent in a day or two." She seemed to have gathered confidence from another look at him, and he was glad he had waited to unpack his town clothes, instead of rushing, as he had first thought of doing, straight from the steamer train to the house. "If it's for something important, I could give you the address,"

160

she finally condescended, apparently reassured by her inspection.

"It *is* important," said the young man almost solemnly; and she handed him a sheet of gold-monogrammed note-paper across which was tumbled, in large loose characters: "Hotel Nouveau Luxe, Paris."

The unexpectedness of the address left Willis French staring. There was nothing to excite surprise in the fact of the Donald Pauls having gone to Paris; or even in their having gone there in their motor; but that they should be lodged at the Nouveau Luxe seemed to sap the very base of probability.

"Are you sure they're staying there?"

To the parlour-maid, at this point, it evidently began to look as if, in spite of his reassuring clothes, the caller might have designs on the umbrellas.

"I couldn't say, sir. It's the address, sir," she returned, adroitly taking her precautions about the door.

These were not lost on the visitor, who, both to tranquillize her and to gain time, turned back toward the quiet Kensington street and stood gazing doubtfully up and down its uneventful length.

All things considered, he had no cause to regret the turn the affair had taken; the only regret he allowed himself was that of not being able instantly to cross the threshold hallowed by his young enthusiasm. But even that privilege might soon be his; and meanwhile he was to have the unforeseen good luck of following Mrs. Donald Paul to Paris. His business in coming to Europe had been simply and solely to see the Donald Pauls; and had they been in London he would have been obliged, their conference over, to return at once to New York, whence he had been sent, at his publisher's expense, to obtain from Mrs. Paul certain details necessary for the completion of his book: *The Art of Horace Fingall*. And now, by a turn of what he fondly called his luck--as if no one else's had ever been quite as rare--he found his vacation prolonged, and his prospect of enjoyment increased, by the failure to meet the lady in London.

Willis French had more than once had occasion to remark that he owed some of his luckiest moments to his failures. He had tried his hand at several of the arts, only to find, in each case, the same impassable gulf between vision and execution; but his ill-success, which he always promptly recognized, had left him leisure to note and enjoy all the incidental compensations of the attempt. And how great some of these compensations were, he had never more keenly felt than on the day when two of the greatest came back to him merged in one glorious opportunity.

It was probable, for example, that if he had drawn a directer profit from his months of study in a certain famous Parisian *atelier*, his labours would have left him less time in which to observe and study Horace Fingall, on the days when the great painter made his round among the students; just as, if he had written better poetry, Mrs. Morland, with whom his old friend Lady Brankhurst had once contrived to have him spend a Sunday in the country, might have given him, during their long confidential talk, less of her sweet compassion and her bracing wisdom. Both Horace Fingall and Emily Morland had, professionally speaking, discouraged their young disciple; the one had said "don't write" as decidedly as the other had said "don't paint"; but both had let him feel that interesting failures may be worth more in the end than dull successes, and that there is range enough for the artistic sensibilities outside the region of production. The fact of the young man's taking their criticism without flinching (as he himself had been thankfully aware of doing) no doubt increased their liking, and thus let him farther into their intimacy. The insight into two such natures seemed, even at the moment, to outweigh any personal success within his reach; and as time removed him from the experience he had less and less occasion to question the completeness of the compensation.

Since then, as it happened, his two great initiators had died within a few months of each other, Emily Morland prematurely, and at the moment when her exquisite art was gaining new warmth from the personal happiness at last opening to her, and Horace Fingall in his late golden prime, when his genius also seemed to be winged for new flights.

Except for the nearness of the two death dates, there was nothing to bring together in the public mind the figures of the painter and the poet, and Willis French's two experiences remained associated in his thoughts only because they had been the greatest revelations of temperament he had ever known. No one but Emily Morland had ever renewed in him that sense of being in the presence of greatness that he had first felt on meeting Horace Fingall. He had often wondered if the only two beings to whom he owed this emotion had ever known each other, and he had concluded that, even in this day of universal meetings, it was unlikely. Fingall, after leaving the United States for Paris toward his fortieth year, had never absented himself from France except on short occasional visits to his native country; and Mrs. Morland, when she at last broke away from her depressing isolation in a Staffordshire parsonage, and set up her own house in London, had been drawn from there only by one or two holiday journeys in Italy. Nothing, moreover, could have been more unlike than the mental quality and the general attitude of the two artists. The only point of resemblance between them lay in the effect they produced of the divine emanation of genius. Willis French's speculations as to the result of a meeting between them had always resulted in the belief that they would not have got on. The two emanations would have neutralized each other, and he suspected that both natures lacked the complementary qualities which might have bridged the gulf between them. And now chance had after all linked their names before posterity, through the fact that the widow of the one had married the man who had been betrothed to the other!...

French's brief glimpses of Fingall and Mrs. Morland had left in him an intense curiosity to know something more of their personal history, and when his publisher had suggested his writing a book on the painter his first thought had been that here was an occasion to obtain the desired light, and to obtain it, at one stroke, through the woman who had been the preponderating influence in Fingall's art, and the man for whom Emily Morland had written her greatest poems.

That Donald Paul should have met and married the widow of Horace Fingall was one of the facts on which young French's imagination had always most appreciatively dwelt. It was strange indeed that these two custodians of great memories, for both of whom any other marriage would have been a derogation, should have found the one way of remaining on the heights; and it was almost equally strange that their inspiration should turn out to be Willis French's opportunity!

At the very outset, the wonder of it was brought home to him by his having to ask for Mrs. Paul at what had once been Mrs. Morland's house. Mrs. Morland had of course bequeathed the house to Donald Paul; and equally of course it was there that, on his marriage to Mrs. Fingall, Donald

Paul had taken his wife. If that wife had been any other, the thought would have been one to shrink from; but to French's mind no threshold was too sacred for the feet of Horace Fingall's widow.

Musing on these things as he glanced up and down the quiet street, the young man, with his sharp professional instinct for missing no chance that delay might cancel, wondered how, before turning from the door, he might get a glimpse of the house which was still--which, in spite of everything, would always be--Emily Morland's.

"You were not thinking of looking at the house, sir?"

French turned back with a start of joy. "Why, yes--I was!" he said instantly.

The parlour-maid opened the door a little wider. "Of course, properly speaking, you should have a card from the agent; but Mrs. Paul *did* say, if anyone was *very* anxious-- May I ask, sir, if you know Mrs. Paul?"

The young man lowered his voice reverentially to answer: "No; but I knew Mrs. Morland."

The parlour-maid looked as if he had misunderstood her question. After a moment's thought she replied: "I don't think I recall the name."

They gazed at each other across incalculable distances, and Willis French found no reply. "What on earth can she suppose I want to see the house for?" he could only wonder.

Her next question told him. "If it's very urgent, sir--"

another glance at the cut of his coat seemed to strengthen her, and she moved back far enough to let him get a foot across the threshold. "Would it be to hire or to buy?"

Again they stared at each other till French saw his own wonder reflected in the servant's doubtful face; then the truth came to him in a rush. The house was not being shown to him because it had once been Emily Morland's and he had been recognized as a pilgrim to the shrine of genius, but because it was Mrs. Donald Paul's and he had been taken for a possible purchaser!

All his disenchantment rose to his lips; but it was checked there by the leap of prudence. He saw that if he showed his wonder he might lose his chance.

"Oh, it would be to buy!" he said; for, though the mere thought of hiring was a desecration, few things would have seemed more possible to him, had his fortune been on the scale of his enthusiasm, than to become the permanent custodian of the house.

The feeling threw such conviction into his words that the parlour-maid yielded another step.

"The drawing-room is this way," she said as he bared his head.

CHAPTER II

It was odd how, as he paced up and down the Embankment late that evening, musing over the vision vouchsafed him, one detail continued to detach itself with discordant sharpness from the harmonious blur.

The parlour-maid who had never heard of Mrs. Morland, and who consequently could not know that the house had ever been hers, had naturally enough explained it to him in terms of its new owners' habits. French's imagination had so promptly anticipated this that he had, almost without a shock, heard Mrs. Morland's library described as "the gentleman's study," and marked how an upstairs sitting-room with faded Venetian furniture and rows of old books in golden-brown calf had been turned, by the intrusion of a large pink toilet-table, into "the lady's dressing-room, sir." It did not offend him that the dwelling should he used as suited the convenience of the persons who lived in it; he was never for expecting life to stop, and the Historic House which has been turned into a show had always seemed to him as dead as a blown egg. He had small patience with the kind of reverence which treats fine things as if their fineness made them useless. Nothing, he thought, was too fine for natural uses, nothing in life too good for life; he liked the absent and unknown Donald Pauls the better for living naturally in this house which had come to them naturally, and not shrinking into the mere keepers of a shrine. But he had winced at just one thing: at seeing there, on the writing-table which had once been Emily Morland's, and must still, he quickly noted, be much as she had left it--at seeing there, among pens and pencils and ink-stained paper-cutters, halfway between a lacquer cup full of elastic bands and a blotting-book with her initials on it, one solitary object of irrelevant newness: an immense expensively framed photograph of Fingall's picture of his wife.

The portrait--the famous first one, now in the Luxembourg--was so beautiful, and so expressive of what lovers of Fingall's art most loved in it, that Willis French was grieved to see it so indelicately and almost insolently out of place. If ever a thing of beauty can give offence, Mrs. Fingall's portrait on Emily Morland's writing-table gave offence. Its presence there shook down all manner of French's faiths. There was something shockingly crude in the way it made the woman in possession triumph over the woman who was gone.

It would have been different, he felt at once, if Mrs. Morland had lived long enough to marry the man she loved; then the dead and the living woman would have faced each other on an equality. But Mrs. Morland, to secure her two brief years of happiness, had had to defy conventions and endure affronts. When, breaking away from the unhappy conditions of her married life, she had at last won London and freedom, it was only to learn that the Reverend

Ambrose Morland, informed of her desire to remarry, and of his indisputable right to divorce her, found himself, on religious grounds, unable to set her free. From this situation she sought no sensational escape. Perhaps because the man she loved was younger than herself, she chose to make no open claim on him, to place no lien on his future; she simply let it be known to their few nearest friends that he and she belonged to each other as completely as a man and woman of active minds and complex interests can ever belong to each other when such life as they live together must be lived in secret. To a woman like Mrs. Morland the situation could not be other than difficult and unsatisfying. If her personal distinction saved her from social slights it could not save her from social subserviences. Never once, in the short course of her love-history, had she been able to declare her happiness openly, or to let it reveal itself in her conduct; and it seemed, as one considered her case, small solace to remember that some of her most moving verse was the expression of that very privation.

At last her husband's death had freed her, and her coming marriage to Donald Paul been announced; but her own health had already failed, and a few weeks later she too was dead, and Donald Paul lost in the crowd about her grave, behind the Morland relations who, rather generously as people thought, came up from Staffordshire for the funeral of the woman who had brought scandal and glory to their name.

So, tragically and inarticulately, Emily Morland's life had gone out; and now, in the house where she and her lover had spent their short secret hours, on the very table at which she had sat and imperishably written down her love, he had put the portrait of the other woman, her successor; the woman to whom had been given the one great thing she had lacked...

Well, that was life too, French supposed: the ceaseless ruthless turning of the wheel! If only--yes, here was where the real pang lay--if only the supplanting face had not been so different from the face supplanted! Standing there before Mrs. Fingall's image, how could he not recall his first sight of Emily Morland, how not feel again the sudden drop of all his expectations when the one woman he had not noticed on entering Lady Brankhurst's drawing-room, the sallow woman with dull hair and a dowdy dress, had turned out to be his immortal? Afterward, of course, when she began to talk, and he was let into the deep world of her eyes, her face became as satisfying as some grave early sculpture which, the imagination once touched by it, makes more finished graces trivial. But there remained the fact that she was what is called plain, and that her successor was beautiful; and it hurt him to see that perfect face, so all-expressive and all-satisfying, in the very spot where Emily Morland, to make her beauty visible, had had to clothe it in poetry. What would she not have given, French wondered, just once to let her face speak for her instead?

The sense of injustice was so strong in him that when he returned to his hotel he went at once to his portmanteau and, pulling out Mrs. Morland's last volume, sat down to reread the famous love-sonnets. It was as if he wanted to make up to her for the slight of which he had been the unwilling witness...

The next day, when he set out for France, his mood had changed. After all, Mrs. Morland had had her compensations. She had been inspired, which, on the whole, is more worth while than to inspire. And then his own adventure was almost in his grasp; and he was at the age when each moment seems to stretch out to the horizon.

The day was fine, and as he sat on the deck of the steamer watching the white cliffs fade, the thought of Mrs. Morland was displaced by the vision of her successor. He recalled the day when Mrs. Fingall had first looked out at him from her husband's famous portrait of her, so frail, so pale under the gloom and glory of her hair, and he had been told how the sight of her had suddenly drawn the painter's genius from its long eclipse. Fingall had found her among the art students of one of the Parisian studios which he fitfully inspected, had rescued her from financial difficulties and married her within a few weeks of their meeting: French had had the tale from Lady Brankhurst, who was an encyclopaedia of illustrious biographies.

"Poor little Bessy Reck--a little American waif sent out from some prairie burrow to 'learn art'--that was literally how she expressed it! She hadn't a relation of her own, I believe: the people of the place she came from had taken pity on her and scraped together enough money for her passage and for two years of the Latin Quarter. After that she was to live on the sale of her pictures! And suddenly she met Fingall, and found out what she was really made for."

So far Lady Brankhurst had been satisfying, as she always was when she trod on solid fact. But she never knew anything about her friends except what had happened to them, and when questioned as to what Mrs. Fingall was really like she became vague and slightly irritable.

"Oh, well, he transformed her, of course: for one thing he made her do her hair differently. Imagine; she used to puff it out over her forehead! And when we went to the studio she was always dressed in the most marvellous Eastern things. Fingall drank cups and cups of Turkish coffee, and she learned to make it herself--it *is* better, of course, but so messy to make The studio was full of Siamese cats. It was somewhere over near the Luxembourg--very picturesque, but one *did* smell the drains. I used always to take my salts with me; and the stairs were pitch-black." That was all.

But from her very omissions French had constructed the vision of something too fine and imponderable not to escape Lady Brankhurst, and had rejoiced in the thought that, of what must have been the most complete of blisses, hardly anything was exposed to crude comment but the stairs which led to it.

Of Donald Paul he had been able to learn even less, though Lady Brankhurst had so many more facts to give. Donald Paul's life lay open for everybody in London to read. He had been first a "dear boy," with a large and eminently respectable family connection, and then a not especially rising young barrister, who occupied his briefless leisure by occasionally writing things for the reviews. He had written an article about Mrs. Morland, and when, soon afterward, he happened to meet her, he had suddenly realized that he hadn't understood her poetry in the least, and had told her so and written another article--under her guidance, the malicious whispered, and boundlessly enthusiastic, of course; people said it was that which had made her fall in love with him. But Lady Brankhurst thought it was more likely to have been his looks--with which French, on general principles, was inclined to agree. "What sort of looks?" he asked. "Oh, like an old picture, you know"; and at that shadowy stage of development the image of Donald Paul had hung. French, in spite of an extensive search, had not even been able to find out where the fateful articles on Mrs. Morland's verse had been published; and light on that point was one of the many lesser results he now hoped for.

Meanwhile, settled in his chair on deck, he was so busy

elaborating his own picture of the couple he was hastening to that he hardly noticed the slim figure of a traveller with a sallow keen face and small dark beard who hovered near, as if for recognition.

"Andre Jolyesse--you don't remember me?" the gentleman at length reminded him in beautifully correct English; and French woke to the fact that it was of course Jolyesse, the eminent international portrait painter, whose expensively gloved hand he was shaking.

"We crossed together on the *Gothic* the last time I went to the States," Monsieur Jolyesse reminded him, "and you were so amiable as to introduce me to several charming persons who added greatly to the enjoyment of my visit."

"Of course, of course," French assented; and seeing that the painter was in need of a listener, the young man reluctantly lifted his rugs from the next chair.

It was because Jolyesse, on the steamer, had been so shamelessly in quest of an article that French, to escape his importunities, had passed him on to the charming persons referred to; and if he again hung about in this way, and recalled himself, it was doubtless for a similarly shameless purpose. But French was more than ever steeled against the celebrating of such art as that of Jolyesse; and, to cut off a possible renewal of the request, he managed--in answer to a question as to what he was doing with himself--to mention casually that he had abandoned art criticism for the writing

175

of books.

The portrait painter was far too polite to let his attention visibly drop at this announcement; too polite, even, not to ask with a show of interest if he might know the subject of the work Mr. French was at the moment engaged on.

"Horace Fingall--*bigre!*" he murmured, as if the aridity of the task impressed him while it provoked his pity. "Fingall--Fingall--" he repeated, his incredulous face smilingly turned to French, while he drew a cigarette from a gold case as flat as an envelope.

French gave back the smile. It delighted him, it gave him a new sense of the importance of his task, to know that Jolyesse, in spite of Fingall's posthumous leap to fame, still took that view of him. And then, with a start of wonder, the young man remembered that the two men must have known each other, that they must have had at least casual encounters in the crowded promiscuous life of the painters' Paris. The possibility was so rich in humour that he was moved to question his companion.

"You must have come across Fingall now and then, I suppose?"

Monsieur Jolyesse shrugged his shoulders. "Not for years. He was a savage--he had no sense of solidarity. And envious--!" The artist waved the ringed hand that held his cigarette. "Could one help it if one sold more pictures than he did? But it was gall and worm-wood to him, poor devil.

Of course he sells *now*--tremendously high, I believe. But that's what happens: when an unsuccessful man dies, the dealers seize on him and make him, a factitious reputation. Only it doesn't last. You'd better make haste to finish your book; that sort of celebrity collapses like a soap-bubble. Forgive me," he added, with a touch of studied compunction, "for speaking in this way of your compatriot. Fingall had aptitudes--immense, no doubt--but no technique, and no sense of beauty; none whatever."

French, rejoicing, let the commentary flow on; he even felt the need to stimulate its flow.

"But how about his portrait of his wife--you must know it?"

Jolyesse flung away his cigarette to lift his hands in protest. "That consumptive witch in the Luxembourg? Ah, *mais non!* She looks like a vegetarian vampire. *Voyez vous, si l'on a beaucoup aimé les femmes--*" the painter's smile was evidently intended to justify his championship of female loveliness. He puffed away the subject with his cigarette smoke, and turned to glance down the deck. "There--by Jove, that's what I call a handsome woman! Over there, with the sable cloak and the brand new travelling-bags. A honeymoon outfit, *hein?* If your poor Fin-gall had had the luck to do *that* kind--! I'd like the chance myself."

French, following his glance, saw that it rested on a tall and extremely elegant young woman who was just settling

177

herself in a deck-chair with the assistance of an attentive maid and a hovering steward: A young man, of equal height and almost superior elegance, strolled up to tuck a rug over her shining boot-tips before seating himself at her side; and French had to own that, at least as a moment's ornament, the lady was worth all the trouble spent on her. She seemed, in truth, framed by nature to bloom from one of Monsieur Jolyesse's canvases, so completely did she embody the kind of beauty it was his mission to immortalize. It was annoying that eyes like forest-pools and a mouth like a tropical flower should so fit into that particular type; but then the object of Monsieur Jolyesse's admiration had the air of wearing her features, like her clothes, simply because they were the latest fashion, and not because they were a part of her being. Her inner state was probably a much less complicated affair than her lovely exterior: it was a state, French guessed, of easy apathetic good-humour, galvanized by the occasional need of a cigarette, and by a gentle enjoyment of her companion's conversation. French had wondered, since his childhood, what the Olympian lovers in fashion-plates found to say to each other. Now he knew. They said (he strolled nearer to the couple to catch it): "Did you wire about reserving a compartment?"; and "I haven't seen my golf-clubs since we came on board": and "I do hope Marshall's brought enough of that new stuff for my face,"--and lastly, after a dreamy pause: "I *know* Gwen gave me a book to read when we started, but I can't think where on earth I've put it."

It was odd too that, handsome and young as they still were (both well on the warm side of forty), this striking couple were curiously undefinably old-fashioned--in just the same way as Jolyesse's art. They belonged, for all their up-to-date attire, to a period before the triumph of the slack and the slouching: it was as if their elegance had pined too long in the bud, and its belated flowering had a tinge of staleness.

French mused on these things while he listened to Jolyesse's guesses as to the class and nationality of the couple, and finally, in answer to the insistent question: "But where do you think they come from?" replied a little impatiently: "Oh, from the rue de la Paix, of course!" He was tired of the subject, and of his companion, and wanted to get back to his thoughts of Horace Fingall.

"Ah, I hope so--then I may run across them yet!" Jolyesse, as he gathered up his bags, shot a last glance at the beauty. "I'll haunt the dressmakers till I find her--she looks as if she spent most of her time with them. And the young man evidently refuses her nothing. You'll see, I'll have her in the next Salon!" He turned back to add: "She might be a compatriot of yours. Women who look as if they came out of the depths of history usually turn out to be from your newest Territory. If you run across her, do say a good word for me. My full lengths are fifty thousand francs now--to Americans."

CHAPTER III

All that first evening in Paris the vision of his book grew and grew in French's mind. Much as he loved the great city, nothing it could give him was comparable, at that particular hour, to the rapture of his complete withdrawal from it into the sanctuary of his own thoughts. The very next day he was to see Horace Fingall's widow, and perhaps to put his finger on the clue to the labyrinth: that mysterious tormenting question of the relation between the creative artist's personal experience and its ideal expression. He was to try to guess how much of Mrs. Fingall, beside her features, had passed into her husband's painting; and merely to ponder on that opportunity was to plunge himself into the heart of his subject. Fingall's art had at last received recognition, genuine from the few, but mainly, no doubt, inspired by the motives to which Jolyesse had sneeringly alluded; and, intolerable as it was to French to think that snobbishness and cupidity were the chief elements in the general acclamation of his idol, he could not forget that he owed to these baser ingredients the chance to utter his own panegyric. It was because the vulgar herd at last wanted to know what to say when it heard Fingall mentioned that Willis French was to be allowed to tell them; such was the base rubble the Temple of Fame was built of! Yes, but future generations would enrich its face with lasting marbles; and it was to be French's privilege to put the first slab in place.

The young man, thus brooding, lost himself in the alluring and perplexing alternatives of his plan. The particular way of dealing with a man's art depended, of course, so much on its relation to his private life, and on the chance of a real insight into that. Fingall's life had been obdurately closed and aloof; would it be his widow's, wish that it should remain so? Or would she understand that any serious attempt to analyse so complex and individual an art must be preceded by a reverent scrutiny of the artist's personality? Would she, above all, understand how reverent French's scrutiny would be, and consent, for the sake of her husband's glory, to guide and enlighten it? Her attitude, of course, as he was nervously aware, would greatly depend on his: on his finding the right words and the convincing tone. He could almost have prayed for guidance, for some supernatural light on what to say to her! It was late that night when, turning from his open window above the throbbing city, he murmured to himself: "I wonder what on earth we shall begin by saying to each other?"

Her sitting-room at the Nouveau Luxe was empty when he was shown into it the next day, though a friendly note had assured him that she would be in by five. But he was not sorry she was late, for the room had its secrets to reveal. The most conspicuous of these was a large photograph of a handsome young man, in a frame which French instantly recognized as the mate of the one he had noticed on Mrs. Morland's writing-table. Well--it was natural, and rather charming, that the happy couple should choose the same frame for each other's portraits, and there was nothing offensive to Fingall's memory in the fact of Donald Paul's picture being the most prominent object in his wife's drawing-room.

Only--if this were indeed Donald Paul, where had French seen him already? He was still questioning the lines of the pleasant oft-repeated face when his answer entered the room in the shape of a splendidly draped and feathered lady.

"I'm so sorry! The dressmakers are such beasts--they've been sticking pins in me ever since two o'clock." She held out her hand with a click of bracelets slipping down to the slim wrist. "Donald! Do come--it's Mr. French," she called back over her shoulder; and the gentleman of the photograph came in after her.

The three stood looking at each other for an interval deeply momentous to French, obviously less stirring to his hosts; then Donald Paul said, in a fresh voice a good deal younger than his ingenuous middle-aged face: "We've met somewhere before, surely. Wasn't it the other day at Brighton--at the Metropole?"

His wife looked at him and smiled, wrinkling her perfect brows a little in the effort to help his memory. "We go to so many hotels! I think it was at the Regina at Harrogate." She appealed to their visitor for corroboration.

"Wasn't it simply yesterday, on the Channel?" French suggested, the words buzzing a little in his own ears; and Mrs. Paul instantly remembered.

"Of course! How stupid of me!" Her random sweetness grew more concentrated. "You were talking to a dark man with a beard--Andre Jolyesse, wasn't it? I told my husband it was Jolyesse. How awfully interesting that you should know him! Do sit down and let me give you some tea while you tell us all about him."

French, as he took the cup from her hand, remembered that, a few hours earlier, he had been wondering what he and she would first say to each other.

It was dark when he walked away from the blazing front of the Nouveau Luxe. Mrs. Donald Paul had given him two generous hours, and had filled them with talk of her first husband; yet as French turned from the hotel he had the feeling that what he brought away with him had hardly added a grain to his previous, knowledge of Horace Fingall. It was perhaps because he was still too blankly bewildered-- or because he had not yet found the link between what had been and what was--that he had been able to sift only so infinitesimal a residue out of Mrs. Paul's abundance. And his first duty, plainly, if he were ever to thread a way through the tangle, was to readjust himself and try to see things from a different point of view.

His one definite impression was that Mrs. Paul was very much pleased that he should have come to Paris to see her, and acutely, though artlessly, aware of the importance of his mission. Artlessness, in fact, seemed her salient quality: there looked out of her great Sphinx-eyes a consciousness as cloudless as a child's. But one thing he speedily discovered: she was keenly alive to her first husband's greatness. On that point French saw that she needed no enlightenment. He was even surprised, sitting opposite to her in all the blatancy of hotel mirrors and gilding, to catch on her lips the echoes of so different a setting. But he gradually perceived that the words she used had no meaning for her save, as it were, a symbolic one: they were like the mysterious price-marks with which dealers label their treasures. She knew that her husband had been proud and isolated, that he had "painted only for himself" and had "simply despised popularity"; but she rejoiced that he was now at last receiving "the kind of recognition even he would have cared for"; and when French, at this point, interposed, with an impulse of self-vindication: "I didn't know that, as yet, much had been written about him that he would have liked," she opened her fathomless eyes a little wider, and answered: "Oh, but the dealers are simply fighting for his things."

The shock was severe; but presently French rallied enough to understand that she was not moved by a spirit of cupidity, but was simply applying the only measure of greatness she knew. In Fingall's lifetime she had learned her lesson, and no doubt repeated it correctly--her conscientious desire for correctness was disarming--but now that he was gone his teaching had got mixed with other formulas, and she was serenely persuaded that, in any art, the proof and corollary of greatness was to become a best seller. "Of course he was his own worst enemy," she sighed. "Even when people *came* to buy he managed to send them away discouraged. Whereas now--!"

In the first chill of his disillusionment French thought for a moment of flight. Mrs. Paul had promised him all the documentation he required: she had met him more than half-way in her lavish fixing of hours and offering of material. But everything in him shrank from repeating the experience he had just been subjected to. What was the use of seeing her again, even though her plans included a visit to Fingall's former studio? She had told him nothing whatever about Fingall, and she had told him only too much about herself. To do that, she had not even had to open her beautiful lips. On his way to her hotel he had stopped in at the Luxembourg, and filled his eyes again with her famous image. Everything she was said to have done for Fingall's genius seemed to burn in the depths of that quiet face. It was like an inexhaustible reservoir of beauty, a still pool into which the imagination could perpetually dip and draw up new treasure. And now, side by side with the painter's vision of her, hung French's own: the vision of the too-smiling beauty set in glasses and glitter, preoccupied with dressmakers and theatre-stalls, and affirming her husband's genius in terms of the auction room and the stock exchange!

"Oh, hang it--what can she give me? I'll go straight back to New York," the young man suddenly resolved. The resolve even carried him precipitately back to his hotel; but on its threshold another thought arrested him. Horace Fingall had not been the only object of his pilgrimage: he had come to Paris to learn what he could of Emily Morland too. That purpose he had naturally not avowed at the Nouveau Luxe: it was hardly the moment to confess his double quest. But the manifest friendliness of Donald Paul convinced him that there would be no difficulty in obtaining whatever enlightenment it was in the young man's power to give. Donald Paul, at first sight, seemed hardly more expressive than his wife; but though his last avatar was one so remote from literature, at least he had once touched its borders and even worn its livery. His great romance had originated in the accident of his having written an article about its heroine; and transient and unproductive as that phase of his experience had probably been, it must have given him a sense of values more applicable than Mrs. Paul's to French's purpose.

Luck continued to favour him; for the next morning, as he went down the stairs of his hotel, he met Donald Paul coming up.

His visitor, fresh and handsome as his photograph, and dressed in exactly the right clothes for the hour and the occasion, held out an eager hand.

"I'm so glad--I hoped I'd catch you," he smiled up at the descending French; and then, as if to tone down what might seem an excess of warmth, or at least make it appear the mere overflow of his natural spirits, he added: "My wife rushed me off to say how sorry she is that she can't take you to the studio this morning. She'd quite forgotten an appointment with her dressmaker--one of her dressmakers!" Donald Paul stressed it with a frank laugh; his desire, evidently, was to forestall French's surprise. "You see," he explained, perhaps guessing that a sense of values was expected of him, "it's rather more of a business for her than for--well, the average woman. These people--the big ones--are really artists themselves nowadays, aren't they? And they all regard her as a sort of Inspiration; she really tries out the coming fashions for them--lots of things succeed or fail as they happen to look on *her*." Here he seemed to think another laugh necessary. "She's always been an Inspiration; it's come to be a sort of obligation to her. You see, I'm sure?"

French protested that he saw--and that any other day was as convenient--

"Ah, but that's the deuce of it! The fact is, we're off for Biarritz the day after to-morrow; and St. Moritz later. We shan't be back here, I suppose, till the early spring. And of course *you* have your plans; ah, going back to America next week? Jove, that is bad." He frowned over it with an artless boyish anxiety. "And tomorrow--well, you know what a woman's last day in Paris is likely to be, when she's had only three of them! Should you mind most awfully--think it hopelessly inadequate, I mean--if I offered to take you to the studio instead?" He reddened a little, evidently not so much at the intrusion of his own person into the setting of his predecessor's life, as at his conscious inability to talk about Horace Fingall in any way that could possibly interest Willis French.

"Of course," he went on, "I shall be a wretched substitute...I know so little...so little in any sense...I never met him," he avowed, as if excusing an unaccountable negligence. "You know how savagely he kept to himself...Poor Bessy--*she* could tell you something about that!" But he pulled up sharp at this involuntary lapse into the personal, and let his smile of interrogation and readiness say the rest for him.

"Go with you? But of course--I shall be delighted," French responded; and a light of relief shone in Mr. Paul's transparent eyes.

"That's very kind of you; and of course she can tell you all about it later--add the details. She told me to say that if you didn't mind turning up again this afternoon late, she'll be ready to answer any questions. Naturally, she's used to that too!"

This sent a slight shiver through French, with its hint of glib replies insensibly shaped by repeated questionings. He knew, of course, that after Fingall's death there had been an outpouring of articles on him in the journals and the art-reviews of every country: to correct their mistakes and fill up their omissions was the particular purpose of his book. But it took the bloom--another layer of bloom--from his enthusiasm to feel that Mrs. Paul's information, meagre as it was, had already been robbed of its spontaneity, that she had only been reciting to him what previous interrogators had been capable of suggesting, and had themselves expected to hear.

Perhaps Mr. Paul read the disappointment in his looks, and misinterpreted it, for he added: "You can't think how I feel the absurdity of trying to talk to *you* about Fingall!"

His modesty was disarming. French answered with sincerity: "I assure you I shall like nothing better than going there with you," and Donald Paul, who was evidently used to assuming that the sentiments of others were as genuine as his own, at once brightened into recovered boyishness.

"That's jolly.--Taxi!" he cried, and they were off.

189

CHAPTER IV

Almost as soon as they entered the flat, French had again to hail the reappearance of his "luck." Better, a thousand times better, to stand in this place with Donald Paul than with Horace Fingall's widow!

Donald Paul, slipping the key into the rusty lock, had opened the door and drawn back to let the visitor pass. The studio was cold and empty--how empty and how cold! No one had lived in the flat since Fingall's death: during the first months following it the widow had used the studio to store his pictures, and only now that the last were sold, or distributed for sale among the dealers, had the place been put in the hands of the agents--like Mrs. Morland's house in Kensington.

In the wintry overhead light the dust showed thick on the rough paint-stained floor, on the few canvases leaning against the walls, and the painter's inconceivably meagre "properties." French had known that Fin-gall's studio would not be the upholstered setting for afternoon teas of Lady Brankhurst's vision, but he had not dared to expect such a scornful bareness. He looked about him reverently.

Donald Paul remained silent; then he gave one of his shy laughs. "Not much in the way of cosy corners, eh? Looks rather as if it had been cleared for a prize fight."

French turned to him. "Well, it *was*. When he wrestled

190

with the Angel until dawn."

Mr. Paul's open gaze was shadowed by a faint perplexity, and for half a second French wondered if his metaphor had been taken as referring to the former Mrs. Fin-gall. But in another moment his companion's eyes cleared. "Of course--I see! Like What's-his-name: in the Bible, wasn't he?" He stopped, and began again impulsively: "I like that idea, you know; he *did* wrestle with his work! Bessy says he used to paint a thing over twenty times--or thirty, if necessary. It drove his sitters nearly mad. That's why he had to wait so long for success, I suppose." His glance seemed to appeal to French to corroborate this rather adventurous view.

"One of the reasons," French assented.

His eyes were travelling slowly and greedily about the vast cold room. He had instantly noted that, in Lady Brankhurst's description of the place, nothing was exact but the blackness of the stairs that led there. The rest she must have got up from muddled memories of other studios--that of Jolyesse, no doubt, among the number. French could see Jolyesse, in a setting of *bibelots*, dispensing Turkish coffee to fashionable sitters. But the nakedness of Fingall's studio had assuredly never been draped: as they beheld it now, so it must have been when the great man painted there--save, indeed, for the pictures once so closely covering the walls (as French saw from the number of empty nails) that to enter it must have been like walking into the heart of a sunset.

191

None were left. Paul had moved away and stood looking out of the window, and timidly, tentatively, French turned around, one after another, the canvases against the wall. All were as bare as the room, though already prepared for future splendours by the hand from which the brush had dropped so abruptly. On one only a few charcoal strokes hinted at a head--unless indeed it were a landscape? The more French looked the less intelligible it became--the mere first stammer of an unuttered message. The young man put it back with a sigh. He would have liked, beyond almost everything, here under Fingall's roof to discover just one of his pictures.

"If you'd care to see the other rooms? You know he and Bessy lived here," he heard his companion suggest.

"Oh, immensely!"

Donald Paul opened a door, struck a match in a dark passage, and preceded him. "Nothing's changed."

The rooms, which were few and small, were still furnished; and this gave French the measure of their humbleness--for they were almost as devoid of comfort as the studio. Fingall must have lived so intensely and constantly in his own inner vision that nothing external mattered. He must have been almost as detached from the visible world as a great musician or a great ascetic; at least till one sat him down before a face or a landscape--and then what he looked at became the whole of the visible world to him.

"Rather doleful diggings for a young woman," Donald

Paul commented with a half-apologetic smile, as if to say: "Can you wonder that she likes the Nouveau Luxe?"

French acquiesced. "I suppose, like all the very greatest of them, he was indifferent to lots of things we think important."

"Yes--and then..." Paul hesitated. "Then they were so frightfully poor. He didn't know how to manage--how to get on with people, either sitters or dealers. For years he sold nothing, literally nothing. It *was* hard on her. She saw so well what he ought to have done; but he wouldn't listen to her!"

"Oh--" French stammered; and saw the other faintly redden.

"I don't mean, of course, that an artist, a great creative artist, isn't always different...on the contrary..." Paul hesitated again. "I understand all that...I've experienced it..." His handsome face softened, and French, mollified, murmured to himself; "He was awfully kind to Emily Morland--I'm sure he was."

"Only," Mrs. Paul's husband continued with a deepening earnestness, as if he were trying to explain to French something not quite clear to himself, "only, if you're not a great creative artist yourself, it is hard sometimes, sitting by and looking on and feeling that if you were just allowed to say a word--. Of course," he added abruptly, "he was very good to her in other ways; very grateful. She was his Inspiration."

"It's something to have been that," French said; and at the words his companion's colour deepened to a flush which took in his neck and ears, and spread up to his white forehead.

"It's everything," he agreed, almost solemnly.

French had wandered up to a book-shelf in what had apparently been Fingall's dressing-room. He had seen no other books about, and was curious to learn what these had to tell him. They were chiefly old Tauchnitz novels--mild mid-Victorian fiction rubbing elbows with a few odd volumes of Dumas, Maupassant and Zola. But under a loose pile the critic, with beating heart, had detected a shabby sketch-book. His hand shook as he opened it; but its pages were blank, and he reflected ironically that had they not been the dealers would never have left it there.

"They've been over the place with a fine-toothcomb," he muttered to himself.

"What have you got hold of?" Donald Paul asked, coming up.

French continued mechanically to flutter the blank pages; then his hand paused at one which was scribbled over with dots and diagrams, and marginal notes in Fingall's small cramped writing.

"Tea-party," it was cryptically entitled, with a date beneath; and on the next page, under the beading: "For tea-party," a single figure stood out--the figure of a dowdily-dressed woman seated in a low chair, a cup in her hand, and looking up as if to speak to some one who was not yet sketched in. The drawing, in three chalks on a gray ground, was rapidly but carefully executed: one of those light and perfect things which used to fall from Fingall like stray petals from a great tree in bloom. The woman's attitude was full of an ardent interest; from the forward thrust of her clumsily-shod foot to the tilt of her head and the high light on her eye-glasses, everything about her seemed electrified by some eager shock of ideas.

"Who was talking to her--and what could he have been saying?" was the first thought the little drawing suggested. But it merely flashed through French's mind, for he had almost instantly recognized the portrait--just touched with caricature, yet living, human, even tender--of the woman he least expected to see there.

"Then she *did* know him!" he triumphed out aloud, forgetting who was at his elbow. He flushed up at his blunder and put the book in his companion's hand.

Donald Paul stared at the page.

"She--who?"

French stood confounded. There she sat--Emily Morland--aquiver in every line with life and sound and colour: French could hear her very voice running up and down its happy scales! And beside him stood her lover, and did not recognize her...

"Oh--" Paul stammered at length. "It's--you mean?" He

looked again. "You think he meant it for Mrs. Morland?" Without waiting for an answer he fixed French with his large boyish gaze, and exclaimed abruptly: "Then you knew her?"

"Oh, I saw her only once--just once." French couldn't resist laying a little stress on the *once*.

But Donald Paul took the answer unresentfully. "And yet you recognized her. I suppose you're more used than I am to Fingall's way of drawing. Do you think he was ever very good at likenesses? I *do* see now, of course...but, come, I call it a caricature, don't you?"

"Oh, what does that matter?"

"You mean, you think it's so clever?"

"I think it's magnificent!" said French with emotion.

The other still looked at him ingenuously, but with a dawning light of eagerness. It recalled to French the suppressed, the exaggerated warmth of his greeting on the hotel stairs. "What is it he wants of me? For he wants something."

"I never knew, either," Paul continued, "that she and Fingall had met. Some one must have brought her here, I suppose. It's curious." He pondered, still holding the book. "And I didn't know you knew her," he concluded.

"Oh, how should you? She was probably unconscious of the fact herself. I spent a day with her once in the country, years ago. Naturally, I've never forgotten it."

Donald Paul's eyes continued obscurely to entreat him.

"That's wonderful!"

"What--that one should never forget having once met Emily Morland?" French rejoined, with a smile he could not repress.

"No," said Emily Morland's lover with simplicity. "But the coincidence. You see, I'd made up my mind to ask you--." He broke off, and looked down at the sketch, as if seeking guidance where doubtless he had so often found it. "The fact is," he began again, "I'm going to write her Life. She left me all her papers--I daresay you know about all that. It's a trust--a sacred trust; but it's also a most tremendous undertaking! And yesterday, after hearing something of what you're planning about Fingall, I realized how little I'd really thought the book out, how unprepared I was--what a lot more there was in that sort of thing than I'd at first imagined. I used to write--a little; just short reviews, and that kind of thing. But my hand's out nowadays; and besides, this is so different. And then, my time's not quite my own any longer...So I made up my mind that I'd consult you, ask you if you'd help me...oh, as much as ever you're willing..." His smile was irresistible. "I asked Bessy. And she thought you'd understand."

"Understand?" gasped French. "Understand?"

"You see," Paul hurried on, "there are heaps and heaps of letters--her beautiful letters! I don't mean--" his voice trembled slightly--"only the ones to me; though some of those...well,

I'll leave it to you to judge...But lots of others too, that all sorts of people have sent me. Apparently everybody kept her letters. And I'm simply swamped in them," he ended helplessly, "unless you will."

French's voice was as unsteady as his. "Unless I will? There's nothing on earth I'd have asked...if I could have imagined it..."

"Oh, really?" Paul's voice dropped back with relief to its everyday tone. He was clearly unprepared for exaltation. "It's amazingly kind of you--so kind that I don't in the least know how to thank you."

He paused, his hand still between the pages of the sketch-book. Suddenly he opened it and glanced down again at the drawing, and then at French.

"Meanwhile--if you really like this thing; you *do?*" He smiled a little incredulously and bent his handsome head to give the leaf a closer look. "Yes, there are his initials; well, that makes it all the more..." He tore out the page and handed it to French. "Do take it," he said. "I wish I had something better of her to give you--but there's literally nothing else; nothing except the beautiful enlarged photograph she had done for me the year we met; and that, of course--"

CHAPTER V

Mrs. Paul, as French had foreseen she would be, was late at their second appointment; later even than at the first. But what did French care? He could have waited contentedly for a week in that blatant drawing-room, with such hopes in his bosom and such a treasure already locked up in his portmanteau. And when at last she came she was just as cordial, as voluble and as unhelpful as ever.

The great difficulty, of course, was that she and her husband were leaving Paris so soon, and that French, for his part, was under orders to return at once to America. "The things I could tell you if we only had the time!" she sighed regretfully. But this left French unmoved, for he knew by now how little she really had to tell. Still, he had a good many more questions to ask, a good many more dates and facts to get at, than could be crowded into their confused hour over a laden tea-table, with belated parcels perpetually arriving, the telephone ringing, and the maid putting in her head to ask if the orange and silver brocade was to go to Biarritz, or to be sent straight on with the furs and the sports clothes to St. Moritz.

Finally, in the hurried parenthesis between these weightier matters, he extracted from her the promise to meet him in Paris in March--March at the latest--and give him a week, a whole week. "It will be so much easier, then, of course," she agreed. "It's the deadest season of the year in Paris. There'll be nobody to bother us, and we can really settle down to work--" her lovely eyes kindled at the thought--"and I can give you all the papers you need, and tell you everything you want to know."

With that he had to be content, and he could afford to be--now. He rose to take leave; but suddenly she rose also, a new eagerness in her eyes. She moved toward the door with him, and there her look detained him.

"And Donald's book too; you can get to work with Donald at the same time, can't you?" She smiled on him confidentially. "He's told me that you've promised to help him out--it's so angelically good of you! I do assure you he appreciates it immensely. Perhaps he's a little too modest about his own ability; but it is a terrible burden to have had imposed on him, isn't it, just as he and I were having our first real holiday! It's been a nightmare to him all these months. Reading all those letters and manuscripts, and deciding--. Why don't authors do those things for themselves?" She appealed to French, half indignantly. "But after all," she concluded, her smile deepening, "I understand that you should be willing to take the trouble, in return for the precious thing he's given you."

French's heart gave a frightened thump: her smile had suddenly become too significant.

"The precious thing?"

She laughed. "Do you mean to say you've forgotten it

already? Well, if you have, I don't think you deserve it. The portrait of Mrs. Morland--the *only* one, apparently A signed drawing of Horace's; it's something of a prize, you'll admit. Donald tells me that you and he made the discovery of the sketch-book together. I can't for the life of me imagine how it ever escaped those harpies of dealers. You can fancy how they went through everything...like detectives after finger-prints, I used to say! Poor me--they used to have me out of bed every day at daylight! How furious they'd be if they knew what they've missed!" She paused and laughed again, leaning in the doorway in one of her long Artemis-attitudes.

French felt his head spinning. He dared not meet her eyes, for fear of discovering in them the unmasked cupidity he fancied he had once before detected there. He felt too sick for any thought but flight; but every nerve in him cried out: "Whatever she says or does, she shall never never have that drawing back!"

She said and did nothing; which made it even more difficult for him. It gave him the feeling that if he moved she would move too--with a spring, as if she herself were a detective, and suspected him of having the treasure in his pocket ("Thank God I haven't!" he thought). And she had him so entirely at her mercy, with all the Fingall dates and documents still in her hold; there was nothing he could do but go--pick up the portmanteau with the drawing in it, and fly by the next train, if need be!

The idea traversed him in a flash, and then gave way again to the desolating sense of who she was, and what it was that they were manoeuvring and watching each other about. That was the worst of all--worse even than giving up the drawing, or renouncing the book on Fingall. He felt that he must get away at any cost, rather than prolong their silent duel; and, sick at heart, he reached out for the door-knob.

"Oh, no!" she exclaimed, her hand coming down on his wrist.

He forced an answering smile. "No?"

She shook her head, her eyes still on his. "You're not going like that." Though she held him playfully her long fine fingers seemed as strong as steel. "After all, business is business, isn't it? We ordinary mortals, who don't live in the clouds among the gods, can't afford to give nothing for nothing... *You* don't--so why should I?"

He had never seen her so close before, and as her face hovered over him, so warm, persuasive, confident, he noted in it, with a kind of savage satisfaction, the first faint lines of age.

"So why should I?" she repeated gaily. He stood silent, imprisoned; and she went on, throwing her head back a little, and letting her gaze filter down on him through her rich lowered lashes: "But I know you'll agree with me that it's only fair. After all, Donald has set you the example. He's given you something awfully valuable in return for the favour you're going to do him--the immense favour. Poor darling--there never was anybody as generous as Donald! Don't be alarmed; I'm not going to ask you to give me a present on *that* scale." She drew herself up and threw back her lids, as if challenging him. "You'd have difficulty in finding one--anybody would!"

French was still speechless, bewildered, not daring to think ahead, and all the while confusedly aware that his misery was feeding some obscure springs of amusement in her.

"In return for the equally immense favour I'm going to do you--coming back to Paris in March, and giving you a whole week--what are you going to give *me?* Have you ever thought about *that?*" she flung out at him; and then, before he could answer: "Oh, don't look so miserable--don't rack your brains over it! I told you I wasn't grasping--I'm not going to ask for anything unattainable. Only, you see--" she paused, her face grown suddenly tender and young again--"you see, Donald wants so dreadfully to have a portrait of me, one for his very own, by a painter he really admires; a *likeness*, simply, you see, not one of those wild things poor Horace used to do of me--and what I want is to beg and implore you to ask Jolyesse if he'll do me. I can't ask him myself: Horace despised his things, and was always ridiculing him, and Jolyesse knew it. It's all very well--but, as I used to tell Horace, success does mean something after all, doesn't it? And no one has been more of a success than Jolyesse--I hear his prices have doubled again. Well, that's a proof, in a way...what's the use of denying it? Only it makes it more difficult for poor me, who can't afford him, even if I dared to ask!" She wrinkled her perfect brows in mock distress. "But if *you* would--an old friend like you--if you'd ask it as a personal favour, and make him see that for the widow of a colleague he ought to make a reduction in his price--really a *big* reduction!--I'm sure he'd do it. After all, it's not my fault if my husband didn't like his pictures. And I should be so grateful to you, and so would Donald."

She dropped French's arm and held out both her shining hands to him. "You *will*--you really will? Oh, you dear good man, you!" He had slipped his hands out of hers, but she caught him again, this time not menacingly but exuberantly.

"If you could arrange it for when I'm here in March, that would be simply perfect, wouldn't it? You can, you think? Oh, bless you! And mind, he's got to make it a full-length!" she called after him joyfully across the threshold.

VELVET EAR-PADS

CHAPTER I

Professor Loring G. Hibbart, of Purewater University, Clio, N. Y., settled himself in the corner of his compartment in the Marseilles-Ventimiglia express, drew his velvet ear-pads from his pocket, slipped them over his ears, and began to think.

It was nearly three weeks since he had been able to indulge undisturbed in this enchanting operation. On the steamer which had brought him from Boston to Marseilles considerable opportunity had in truth been afforded him, for though he had instantly discovered his fellow-passengers to be insinuating and pervasive, an extremely rough passage had soon reduced them to inoffensiveness. Unluckily the same cause had in like manner affected the Professor; and when the ship approached calmer waters, and he began to revive, the others revived also, and proceeded to pervade, to insinuate and even to multiply--since a lady gave birth to twins as they entered the Mediterranean.

As for the tumultuous twenty-four hours since his landing, the Professor preferred not to include them in his retrospect. It was enough that they were over. "All I want is *quiet*," he had said to the doctors who, after his alarming attack of influenza, followed by bronchial pneumonia, had ordered an immediate departure for warmer climes; and they had thrust him onto an excursion-steamer jammed with noisy sight-seers, and shipped him to a port whither all the rest of the world appeared to be bound at the same moment! His own fault, perhaps? Well--he never could plan or decide in a hurry, and when, still shaken by illness, he had suddenly been told that he must spend six months in a mild climate, and been faced with the alternatives of southern California or southern France, he had chosen the latter because it meant a more complete escape from professional associations and the terror of meeting people one knew. As far as climate went, he understood the chances to be equal; and all he wanted was to recover from his pulmonary trouble and employ his enforced leisure in writing a refutation of Einstein's newly published book on Relativity.

Once the Professor had decided on the south of France, there remained the difficulty of finding, in that populous region, a spot quiet enough to suit him; but after much anxious consultation with colleagues who shared his dread of noise and of promiscuous human intercourse, he had decided on a secluded *pension* high up in the hills, between Monte Carlo and Mentone. In this favoured spot, he was told, no dogs barked, cocks crew or cats courted. There were no waterfalls, or other sonorous natural phenomena, and it was utterly impossible for a motor (even with its muffler knocked off) to ascend the precipitous lane which led to the *pension*. If, in short, it were possible to refute Einstein's theory, it was in just such a place, and there only, that the feat might be accomplished.

Once settled in the train, the Professor breathed more freely. Most of his fellow-passengers had stayed on the ship, which was carrying them on to swarm over a succession of other places as he had just left them swarming over Marseilles. The train he got into was not very crowded, and should other travellers enter the compartment, his ear-pads would secure him from interruption. At last he could revert to the absorbing thought of the book he was planning; could plunge into it like a diver into the ocean. He drew a deep breath and plunged...

Certainly the compartment had been empty when the train left Marseilles--he was sure of that; but he seemed to remember now that a man had got in at a later station, though he couldn't have said where or when; for once he began to think, time vanished from him as utterly as space.

He became conscious of the intruding presence only from the smell of tobacco gradually insinuating itself into his nostrils. Very gradually; for when the Professor had withdrawn into his inner stronghold of Pure Reason, and pulled up the ladder, it was not easy for any appeal to reach him through the channel of the senses. Not that these were defective in him. Far from it: he could smell and see, taste and hear, with any man alive; but for many years past he had refrained from exercising these faculties except in so far as they conduced to the maintenance of life and security. He would have preferred that the world should contain nothing to see, nothing to smell, nothing to hear; and by negativing persistently every superfluous hint of his visual, auditive or olfactory organs he had sheathed himself in a general impenetrability of which the ear-pads were merely a restricted symbol.

His noticing the whiff of tobacco was an accident, a symptom of his still disorganized state; he put the smell resolutely from him, registered "A Man Opposite," and plunged again into the Abstract.

Once--about an hour later, he fancied--the train stopped with a jerk which flung him abruptly out of his corner. His mental balance was disturbed, and for one irritating instant his gaze unwillingly rested on silver groves, purple promontories and a blue sea. "Ugh--*scenery!*" he muttered; and with a renewed effort of the will he dropped his mental curtain between that inconsequent jumble of phenomena and the absolutely featureless area in which the pure intellect thrones. The incident had brought back the smell of his neighbour's cigarette; but the Professor sternly excluded that also, and the train moved on...

Professor Hibbart was in truth a man of passionately excitable nature: no one was ever, by temperament, less adapted to the lofty intellectual labours in which his mind delighted. He asked only to live in the empyrean; but he was perpetually being dragged back to earth by the pity, wrath or contempt excited in him by the slipshod course of human affairs. There were only two objects on which he flattered himself he could always look with a perfectly unseeing eye; and these were a romantic landscape and a pretty woman. And he was not absolutely sure about the landscape.

Suddenly a touch, soft yet peremptory, was laid on his arm. Looking down, he beheld a gloved hand; looking up he saw that the man opposite him was a woman.

To this awkward discovery he was still prepared to oppose the blank wall of the most complete imperception. But a sharp pinch proved that the lady who had taken hold of his arm had done so with the fixed determination to attract his attention, at the cost of whatever pain or inconvenience to himself. As she appeared also to be saying something-- probably asking if the next station were the one at which she ought to get out--he formed with soundless lips the word "Deaf," and pointed to his ears. The lady's reply was to release his wrist, and with her free hand flick off an ear-pad.

"Deaf? Oh, no," she said briskly, in fluent but exotic English. "You wouldn't need ear-pads if you were. You don't want to be bothered--that's all. I know the trick; you got it out of Herbert Spencer!"

The assault had nearly disabled the Professor for farther resistance; but he rallied his wits and answered stonily: "I have no time-table. You'd better consult the guard."

The lady threw her spent cigarette out of the window. As the smoke drifted away from her features he became uneasily aware that they were youthful, and that the muscles about her lips and eyes were contracted into what is currently known as a smile. In another moment, he realized with dismay, he was going to know what she looked like. He averted his eyes.

"I don't want to consult the guard--I want to consult *you*," said the lady.

His ears took reluctant note of an intonation at once gay and appealing, which caressed the "You" as if it were a new pronoun rich in vowels, and the only one of its kind in the world.

"Eeee-you," she repeated.

He shook his averted head. "I don't know the name of a single station on this line."

"Dear me, don't you?" The idea seemed to shock her, to make a peculiar appeal to her sympathy. "But I do--every one of them! With my eyes shut. Listen: I'll begin at the beginning. Paris--"

"But I don't *want* to know them!" he almost screamed.

"Well, neither do I. What I want is to ask you a favour--just one tiny little enormous favour."

The Professor still looked away. "I have been in very bad health until recently," he volunteered.

"Oh, I'm so glad--glad, I mean," she corrected herself

hastily, "that you're all right again now! And glad too that you've been ill, since that just confirms it--"

Here the Professor fell. "Confirms what?" he snapped, and saw too late the trap into which he had plunged.

"My belief that you are predestined to help me," replied his neighbour with joyful conviction.

"Oh, but that's quite a mistake--a complete mistake. I never in my life helped anybody, in any way. I've always made it a rule not to."

"Not even a Russian refugee?"

"Never!"

"Oh, yes, you have. You've helped *me!*"

The Professor turned an ireful glance upon her, and she nodded. "I am a Russian refugee."

"You?" he exclaimed. His eyes, by this time, had definitely escaped from his control, and were recording with an irrepressible activity and an exasperating precision the details of her appearance and her dress. Both were harmonious and opulent. He laughed incredulously.

"Why do you laugh? Can't you see that I'm a refugee; by my clothes, I mean? Who has such pearls but Russian refugees? Or such sables? We have to have them--to sell, of course You don't care to buy my sables, do you? For you they would be only six thousand pounds cash. No, I thought not. It's my duty to ask--but I didn't suppose they would interest you. The Paris and London jewellers farm out the pearls to us; the big dressmakers supply the furs. For of course we've all sold the originals long ago. And really I've been rather successful. I placed two sets of silver fox and a rope of pearls last week at Monte Carlo. Ah, that fatal place! I gambled away the whole of my commission the same night...But I'm forgetting to tell you how you've already helped me..."

She paused to draw breath, and in the pause the Professor, who had kept his hand on his loosened ear-pad, slipped it back over his ear.

"I wear these," he said coldly, "to avoid argument."

With a flick she had it off again. "I wasn't going to argue--I was only going to thank you."

"I can't conceive for what. In any case, I don't want to be thanked."

Her brows gathered resentfully. "Why did you *ask* to be, then?" she snapped; and opening a bejewelled wrist-bag she drew forth from a smother of cigarette-papers and pawn-tickets a slip of paper on which her astonished companion read a phrase written in a pointed feminine hand, but signed with his own name.

" *There!*"

The Professor took the paper and scanned it indignantly. "This copy of 'The Elimination of Phenomena' was presented by Professor Loring G. Hibbart of Purewater University, Clio, N. Y., to the library of the American Y. M. C. A. Refugee Centre at Odessa.

"A word of appreciation, sent by any reader to the above address, would greatly gratify Loring G. Hibbart."

"*There!*" she repeated. "Why did you ask to be thanked if you didn't want to be? What else does 'greatly gratify' mean? I couldn't write to you from Odessa because I hadn't the money to buy a stamp; but I've longed ever since to tell you what your book did for me. It simply changed my whole life--books do sometimes, you know. I saw everything differently--even our Refugee Centre! I decided at once to give up my lover and divorce my husband. Those were my two first Eliminations." She smiled retrospectively. "But you mustn't think I'm a frivolous person. I have my degree as a Doctor of Philosophy--I took it at sixteen, at the University of Moscow. I gave up philosophy the year after for sculpture; the next year I gave up sculpture for mathematics and love. For a year I loved. After that I married Prince Balalatinsky. He was my cousin, and enormously wealthy. I need not have divorced him, as it turned out, for he was soon afterward buried alive by the Bolsheviks. But how could I have foreseen it? And your book had made me feel--"

"Good gracious!" the author of the book interrupted desperately. "You don't suppose *I* wrote that rubbish about wanting to be thanked, do you?"

"Didn't you? How could I tell? Almost all the things sent from America to the refugee camp came with little labels like that. You all seemed to think we were sitting before perfectly appointed desks, with fountain pens and stamp-cases from Bond Street in our pockets. I remember once getting a lip-stick and a Bernard Shaw calendar labelled: 'If the refugee who receives these would write a line of thanks to little Sadie Burt of Meropee Junction, Ga., who bought them out of her own savings by giving up chewing-gum for a whole month, it would make a little American girl very happy.' Of course I was sorry not to be able to write to little Sadie." She broke off, and then added: "Do you know, I was sure you were my Professor as soon as I saw your name on your suit-case?"

"Good Lord!" groaned the Professor.

He had forgotten to remove the obligatory steamer-labels! Instinctively he reached out a hand to tear off the offending member; but again a gesture of the Princess's arrested him. "It's too late now. And you can't surely grudge me the pleasure of thanking you for your book?"

"But I *didn't* ask--"

"No; but I wanted to. You see, at that time I had quite discarded philosophy. I was living in the Actual--with a young officer of Preobrajensky--when the war broke out. And of course in our camp at Odessa the Actual was the very thing one wanted to get away from. And your book took me straight back into that other world where I had known my only pure happiness. Purity--what a wonderful thing it is! What a pity it is so hard to keep; like money, and everything else really valuable! But I'm thankful for any little morsel of it that I've had. When I was only ten years old--"

But suddenly she drew back and nestled down into her lustrous furs. "You thought I was going to tell you the story of my life? No. Put your ear-pads on again. I know now why you wear them--because you're planning a new book. Is it not so? You see I can read your thoughts. Go on--do! I would rather assist at the birth of a masterpiece than chatter about my own insignificant affairs."

The Professor smiled. If she thought masterpieces were born in that way--between railway stations, and in a whirl of prattle I Yet he was not wholly angry. Either because it had been unexpectedly agreeable to hear his book praised, or because of that harmonious impression which, now that he actually saw her, a protracted scrutiny confirmed, he began to feel more tolerantly toward his neighbour. Deliberately, his eyes still on hers, he pushed the other ear-pad away.

"Oh--" she said with a little gasp. "Does that mean I may go on talking?" But before he could answer, her face clouded. "I know--it only means that I might as well, now that I've broken in on your meditations. I'm dreadfully penitent; but luckily you won't have me for long, for I'm getting out at Cannes, and Cannes is the next station. And that reminds me of the enormous little favour I have to ask."

The Professor's face clouded also: he had a nervous apprehension of being asked favours. "My fountain pen," he said, regaining firmness of tone, "is broken."

215

"Ah--you thought I meant to ask for your autograph? Or perhaps for a cheque?" (Lord, how quick she was!) She shook her head. "No, I don't care for compulsory autographs. And I'm not going to ask for money--I'm going to give you some."

He faced her with renewed dismay. Could it be--? After all, he was not more than fifty-seven; and the blameless life he had led had perhaps helped to preserve a certain...at least that was *one* theory...In these corrupt European societies what might a man not find himself exposed to? With some difficulty he executed a pinched smile.

"*Money?*"

She nodded again. "Oh, don't laugh! Don't think I'm joking. It's your ear-pads," she disconcertingly added.

"Yes. If you hadn't put them on I should never have spoken to you; for it wasn't till afterward that I saw your name on the suitcase. And after that I should have been too shy to break in on the meditations of a Great Philosopher. But you see I have been watching--oh, for years!--for your ear-pads."

He stared at her helplessly. "You want to buy them from me?" he asked in terror, wondering how on earth he would be able to get others in a country of which he did not speak the language.

She burst into a laugh that ran up and down the whole scale of friendly derision and tender mockery.

"Buy them? Gracious, no! I could make myself a better

216

pair in five minutes." She smiled at his visible relief. "But you see I'm ruined--stony broke; isn't that what they call it? I have a young American friend who is always saying that about himself. And once in the Caucasus, years ago, a gipsy told me that if ever I had gambled away my last penny (and I nearly *have*) it would all be won back by a pale intellectual looking man in velvet ear-pads, if only I could induce him to put a stake on the tables for me." She leaned forward and scrutinized him. "You are very pale, you know," she said, "and very intellectual looking. I was sure it was you when you told me you'd been ill."

Professor Loring D. Hibbart looked about him desperately. He knew now that he was shut up with a madwoman. A harmless one, probably; but what if, in the depths of that jewelled bag, a toy revolver lurked under the pawn-tickets and the cigarette papers? The Professor's life had been so guarded from what are known as "exciting situations" that he was not sure of his ability to meet one with becoming tact and energy.

"I suppose I'm a physical coward," he reflected bitterly, an uncomfortable dampness breaking out all over him. "And I *know*," he added in self-extenuation, "that I'm in no condition yet for any sort of a struggle..."

But what did one do with lunatics? If only he could remember! And suddenly he did: one humoured them!

Fortified by the thought, he made shift to glance more

kindly toward the Princess Balalatinsky. "So you want me to gamble for you?" he said, in the playful tone he might have adopted in addressing little Sadie Burt of Meropee.

"Oh, how glorious of you! You will? I *knew* you would! But first," she broke off, "you must let me explain--"

"Oh, do explain, of course," he agreed, rapidly calculating that her volubility might make the explanation last until they reached the next station, where, as she had declared, she was to leave the train.

Already her eye was less wild; and he drew an inward breath of relief.

"You angel, you! I *do*," she confessed, "simply love to talk about myself. And I'm sure you'll be interested when I tell you that, if you'll only do as I ask, I shall be able to marry one of your own compatriots--such a beautiful heroic youth! It is for him, for him only, that I long to be wealthy again. If you loved, could you bear to see your beloved threatened with starvation?"

"But I thought," he gently reminded her, "that it was you who were threatened with starvation?"

"We *both* are. Isn't it terrible? You see, when we met and loved, we each had the same thought--to make the other wealthy! It was not possible, at the moment, for either of us to attain our end by the natural expedient of a rich marriage with reasonable prospect of a quick divorce--so we staked our all at those accursed tables, and we both lost! My poor betrothed has only a few hundred francs left, and as for me, I have had to take a miserably paid job as a dressmaker's *mannequin* at Cannes. But I see you are going on to Monte Carlo (yes, that's on your luggage too); and as I don't suppose you will spend a night there without visiting the rooms, I--" She was pulling forth the hundred francs from her inexhaustible bag when the Professor checked her with dismay. Mad though she might be, he could not even make believe to take her money.

"I'm *not* spending a night at Monte Carlo," he protested. "I'm only getting out there to take a motorbus for a quiet place up in the hills; I've the name written down somewhere; my room is engaged, so I couldn't possibly wait over," he argued gently.

She looked at him with what seemed to his inflamed imagination the craftiness of a maniac. "Don't you know that our train is nearly two hours late? I don't suppose you noticed that we ran over a crowded excursion charabanc near Toulon? Didn't you even hear the ambulances rushing up? Your motorbus will certainly have left Monte Carlo when you arrive, so you'll *have* to spend the night there! And even if you don't," she added persuasively, "the station's only two steps from the Casino, and you surely can't refuse just to nip in for half an hour." She clasped her hands in entreaty. "You wouldn't refuse if you knew my betrothed--your young compatriot! If only we had a few thousands all would go smoothly. We should be married at once and go to live on his ancestral estate of Kansas. It appears the climate is that of Africa in summer and of the Government of Omsk in winter; so our plan is to grow oranges and breed sables. You see, we can hardly fail to succeed with two such crops. All we ask is enough money to make a start. And that you will get for me tonight. You have only to stake this hundred franc note; you'll win on the first turn, and you'll go on winning. You'll see!"

With one of her sudden plunges she pried open his contracted fist and pressed into it a banknote wrapped in a torn envelope. "Now listen; this is my address at Cannes. Princess Balala--oh, here's the station. Goodbye, guardian angel. No, "au revoir"; I shall see you soon. They call me Betsy at the dressmaker's..."

Before he could open his convulsed fingers, or dash out after her, she had vanished, bag and baggage, in the crowd and confusion of the platform; other people, pushing and chattering and tearing themselves from the embrace of friends, had piled into her place, and were waving from the window, and blocking the way out; and now the train was moving on, and there he sat in his corner, aghast, clutching the banknote...

CHAPTER II

At Monte Carlo the Professor captured a porter and rescued his luggage. Exhausted by this effort, and by the attempt to communicate with the porter, first in Latin and then in French as practised at Purewater, he withdrew to a corner of the waiting-room and fished in his pockets for the address of the quiet *pension* in the hills. He found it at last, and handed it wearily to the porter. The latter threw up his hands. "*Parti! Parti! Autobus* gone." That devil of a woman had been right!

When would there be another, the Professor asked.

Not till tomorrow morning at 8:30. To confirm his statement the porter pointed to a large time-table on the wall of the waiting-room. The Professor scanned it and sat down again with a groan. He was about to consult his companion as to the possibility of finding a night's lodging in a respectable *pension* (fantastic as the idea seemed in such a place); but hardly had he begun: "Can you tell me where--" when, with a nod of comprehension and a wink of complicity, the porter returned in fluent English: "Pretty ladies? Turkish bath? Fottographs?"

The Professor repudiated these suggestions with a shudder, and leaving his bags in the cloak-room set forth on his quest. He had hardly taken two steps when another stranger of obviously doubtful morality offered him a pamphlet which he was indignantly rejecting when he noticed its title:

"The Theory of Chance in Roulette." The theory of chance was deeply interesting to the Professor, and the idea of its application to roulette not without an abstract attraction. He bought the pamphlet and sat down on the nearest bench.

His study was so absorbing that he was roused only by the fall of twilight, and the scattered twinkle of many lamps all radiating up to the central focus of the Casino. The Professor started to his feet, remembering that he had still to find a lodging. "And I must be up early to catch the bus," he reminded himself. He took his way down a wide empty street apparently leading to a quieter and less illuminated quarter. This street he followed for some distance, vainly scrutinizing the houses, which seemed all to be private dwellings, till at length he ran against a slim well-set-up young fellow in tennis flannels, with a bright conversational eye, who was strolling along from the opposite direction.

"Excuse me, sir," said the Professor.

"What for?" rejoined the other, in a pleasant tone made doubly pleasant by the familiar burr of the last word, which he pronounced like *fur*.

"Why, you're an American!" exclaimed the Professor.

"Sher*lock!*" exulted the young man, extending his hand. "I diagnose the same complaint in yourself."

The Professor sighed pleasurably. "Oh, yes. What I want," he added, "is to find a plain quiet boarding-house or family hotel."

"Same as mother used to make 'em?" The young man reflected. "Well, it's a queer place in which to prosecute your search; but there is one at Monte, and I'm about the only person that knows it. My name's Taber Tring. Come along."

For a second the Professor's eye rested doubtfully on Mr. Tring. He knew, of course--even at Purewater it was known--that in the corrupt capitals of Europe one could not always rely implicitly on the information given by strangers casually encountered; no, not even when it was offered with affability, and in the reassuring twang of the Western States. But after all Monte Carlo was not a capital; it was just an absurd little joke of a town crammed on a ledge between sea and mountain; and a second glance at the young man convinced the Professor that he was as harmless as the town.

Mr. Tring, who seemed quick at thought-reading, returned his look with an amused glance.

"Not much like our big and breezy land, is it? These Riviera resorts always remind me of the subway at rush hours; everybody strap-hanging. But my landlady is an old friend, and I know one of her boarders left this morning, because I heard her trying to seize his luggage. He got away; so I don't see why you shouldn't have his room. See?"

The Professor saw. But he became immediately apprehensive of having his own luggage seized, an experience unprecedented in his history.

"Are such things liable to occur in this place?" he

enquired.

"What? A scrap with your landlady? Not if you pay up regularly; or if she likes you. I guess she didn't like that other fellow; and I know he was always on the wrong side of the tables."

"The tables--do you refer to the gambling tables?" The Professor stopped short to put the question.

"That's it," said the other.

"And do you yourself sometimes visit the gambling-rooms?" the Professor next enquired.

"Oh, hell," said Taber Tring expressively.

The Professor scrutinized him with growing interest. "And have you a theory of chance?"

The young man met his gaze squarely. "I have; but it can't be put into language that would pass the censor."

"Ah--you refer, no doubt, to your personal experience. But, as regards the theory--"

"Well, the theory has let me down to bedrock; and I came down on it devilish hard." His expression turned from apathy to animation. "I'm stony broke; but if you'd like to lend me a hundred francs to have another try--"

"Oh, no," said the Professor hastily; "I don't possess it." And his doubts began to stir again.

Taber Tring laughed. "Of course you don't; not for lending purposes. I was only joking; everybody makes that joke here. Well, here's the house; I'll go ahead and rout out our hostess."

They stopped before a pleasant-looking little house at the end of the street. A palm-tree, a couple of rose-bushes and a gateway surmounted by the word *Arcadie* divided it from the pavement; the Professor drew a breath of relief as a stout lady in an orange wig bustled out to receive him.

In spite of the orange wig her face was so full of a shrewd benevolence that the Professor felt sure he had reached a haven of rest. She welcomed him affably, informed him that she had a room, and offered to lead him up to it. "Only for tonight, though? For it is promised to a Siamese nobleman for tomorrow."

This, the Professor assured her, made no difference, as he would be leaving at daylight. But on the lowest step of the stair he turned and addressed himself to Mr. Tring.

"Perhaps the lady would be good enough to have my bags brought up from the station? If you would kindly explain that I'm going out now to take a little stroll. As I'm leaving so early tomorrow it's my only chance to have a look around."

"That's so; I'll tell her," the young man rejoined sympathetically; and as the Professor's hand was on the gate, he heard Mr. Tring call out, mimicking the stentorian tones of a megaphone man on a sight-seeing motorbus: "Third street to the left, then first right to the tables"; after which he added, in his natural tone: "Say, Arcadia locks up at midnight."

The Professor smiled at the superfluous hint.

CHAPTER III

Having satisfied a polyglot door-keeper as to his nationality, and the fact that he was not a minor, the Professor found himself in the gambling-rooms. They were not particularly crowded for people were beginning to go out for dinner, and he was able to draw fairly near to the first roulette table he encountered.

As he stood looking over the shoulders of the players he understood that no study of abstract theories could be worth the experience acquired by thus observing the humours of the goddess in her very temple. Her caprices, so ably seconded by the inconceivable stupidity, timidity or rashness of her votaries, first amused and finally exasperated the Professor; he began to feel toward her something of the annoyance excited in him by the sight of a pretty woman, or any other vain superfluity, combined with the secret sense that if he chose he could make her dance to his tune, and that it might be mildly amusing to do so. He had felt the same once or twice--but only for a fugitive instant--about pretty women.

None, however, had ever attracted him as strongly as this veiled divinity. The longing to twitch the veil from her cryptic features became violent, irresistible. "Not one of these fools has any idea of the theory of chance," he muttered to himself, elbowing his way to a seat near one of the croupiers. As he did so, he put his hand into his pocket, and found to

227

his disgust that it contained only a single five franc piece and a few *sous*. All the rest of his money--a matter of four or five hundred francs--lay locked up in his suit-case at *Arcadie*. He anathematized his luck in expurgated language, and was about to rise from the table when the croupier called out: "*Faites vos jeux, Messieurs.*"

The Professor, with a murmured expletive which was to a real oath what Postum is to coffee, dropped back into his place and flung his five franc piece on the last three numbers. He lost.

Of course--in his excitement he had gone exactly contrary to his own theory! It was on the first three that he had meant to stake his paltry bet. Well; now it was too late. But stay--

Diving into another pocket, he came with surprise on a hundred franc note. Could it really be his? But no; he had an exact memorandum of his funds, and he knew this banknote was not to be thus accounted for. He made a violent effort to shake off his abstraction, and finally recalled that the note in question had been pressed into his hand that very afternoon as he left the train. But by whom--?

"*Messieurs, faites vos jeux! Faites vos jeux! Le jeu est fait. Rien ne va plus.*"

The hundred francs, escaping from his hand, had fluttered of themselves to a number in the middle of the table. That number came up. Across the green board thirty-six other hundred franc notes flew swiftly back in the direction of the

Professor. Should he put them all back on the same number? "Yes," he nodded calmly to the croupier's question; and the three-thousand seven hundred francs were guided to their place by the croupier's rake.

The number came up again, and another argosy of notes sailed into the haven of the happy gambler's pocket. This time he knew he ought to settle down quietly to his theory; and he did so. He staked a thousand and tripled it, then let the three thousand lie, and won again. He doubled that stake, and began to feel his neighbours watching him with mingled interest and envy as the winnings once more flowed his way. But to whom did this mounting pile really belong?

No time to think of that now; he was fast in the clutches of his theory. It seemed to guide him like some superior being seated at the helm of his intelligence: his private daemon pitted against the veiled goddess! It was exciting, undoubtedly; considerably more so, for example, than taking tea with the President's wife at Purewater. He was beginning to feel like Napoleon, disposing his battalions to right and left, advancing, retreating, reinforcing or redistributing his troops. Ah, the veiled goddess was getting what she deserved for once!

At a late hour of the evening, when the Professor had become the centre of an ever-thickening crowd of fascinated observers, it suddenly came back to him that a woman had given him that original hundred franc note. A woman in the train that afternoon...But what did he care for that? He was playing the limit at every stake; and his mind had never worked more clearly and with a more exquisite sense of complete detachment. He was in his own particular seventh heaven of lucidity. He even recalled, at the precise moment when cognizance of the fact became useful, that the doors of *Arcadie* closed at midnight, and that he had only just time to get back if he wished to sleep with a roof over his head.

As he did wish to, he pocketed his gains quietly and composedly, rose from the table and walked out of the rooms. He felt hungry, cheerful and alert. Perhaps, after all, excitement had been what he needed--pleasurable excitement, that is, not the kind occasioned by the small daily irritations of life, such as the presence of that woman in the train whose name he was still unable to remember. What he would have liked best of all would have been to sit down in one of the brightly lit cafés he was passing, before a bottle of beer and a ham sandwich; or perhaps what he had heard spoken of as a Welsh rabbit. But he did not want to sleep on a bench, for the night air was sharp; so he continued self-denyingly on his way to *Arcadie*.

A sleepy boy in a dirty apron let him in, locked up after him, and led him to a small bare room on the second floor. The stairs creaked and rattled as they mounted, and the rumblings of sleep sounded through the doors of the rooms they passed. *Arcadie* was a cramped and ramshackle construction, and the Professor hoped to heaven that his *pension* in the hills would be more solidly built and less densely inhabited. However, for one night it didn't matter-- or so he imagined.

His guide left him, and he turned on the electric light, threw down on the table the notes with which all his pockets were bulging, and began to unstrap his portmanteaux.

Though he had so little luggage he always found the process of unpacking a long and laborious one; for he never could remember where he had put anything, and invariably passed through all the successive phases of apprehension and despair before he finally discovered his bedroom slippers in his spongebag, and the sponge itself (still dripping) rolled up inside his pyjamas.

But tonight he sought for neither sponge not pyjamas, for as he opened his first suitcase his hand lit on a ream of spotless foolscap--the kind he always used for his literary work. The table on which he had tossed his winnings held a crusty hotel inkstand, and was directly overhung by a vacillating electric bulb. Before it was a chair; through the open window flowed the silence of the night, interwoven with the murmurs of a sleeping sea and hardly disturbed by the occasional far-off hoot of a motor horn. In his own brain was the same nocturnal quiet and serenity. A curious thing had happened to him. His bout with the veiled goddess had sharpened his wits and dragged him suddenly and completely out of

231

the intellectual apathy into which he had been gradually immersed by his illness and the harassing discomforts of the last few weeks. He was no longer thinking now about the gambling tables or the theory of chance; but with all the strength of his freshly stimulated faculties was grappling the mighty monster with whom he meant to try a fall.

"*Einstein!*" he cried, as a Crusader might have shouted his battle-cry. He sat down at the table, shoved aside the banknotes, plunged his pen into the blue mud of the inkstand, and began.

The silence was delicious, mysterious. Link by link the chain of his argument unrolled itself, travelling across his pages with the unending flow of a trail of migratory caterpillars. Not a break; not a hesitation. It was years since his mental machinery had worked with that smooth consecutiveness. He began to wonder whether, after all, it might not be better to give up the idea of a remote and doubtful *pension* in the hills, and settle himself for the winter in a place apparently so propitious to his intellectual activities.

It was then that the noises in the next room suddenly began. First there was the brutal slam of the door, followed by a silly bad-tempered struggle with a reluctant lock. Then a pair of shoes were flung down on the tiled floor. Water was next poured into an unsteady basin, and a water-jug set down with a hideous clatter on a rickety washstand which seemed to be placed against the communicating door between the two rooms. Turbulent ablutions ensued. These over, there succeeded a moment of deceptive calm, almost immediately succeeded by a series of whistled scales, emitted just above the whistler's breath, and merging into the exact though subdued reproduction of various barn-yard gutturals, ending up with the raucous yelp of a parrot proclaiming again and again: "I'm stony broke, I am!"

All the while Professor Hibbart's brain continued to marshal its arguments, and try to press them into the hard mould of words. But the struggle became more and more unequal as the repressed cacophony next door increased. At last he jumped up, rummaged in every pocket for his ear-pads and snapped them furiously over his ears. But this measure, instead of silencing the tenuous insistent noises from the next room, only made him strain for them more attentively through the protecting pads, giving them the supernatural shrillness of sounds heard at midnight in a sleeping house, the secret crackings and creakings against which heaped-up pillows and drawn-up bedclothes are a vain defence.

Finally the Professor noticed that there was a wide crack under the communicating door. Not till that crack was filled would work be possible. He jumped up again and dived at the washstand for towels. But he found that in the hasty preparation of the room the towels had been forgotten. A newspaper, then--but no; he cast about him in vain for a newspaper...

The noises had now sunk to a whisper, broken by irritating intervals of silence; but in the exasperated state of the Professor's nerves these irregular lulls, and the tension of watching for the sounds that broke them, were more trying than what had gone before. He sent a despairing glance about him, and his eye lit on the pile of banknotes on the table. He sprang up again, seized the notes, and crammed them into the crack.

After that the silence became suddenly and almost miraculously complete, and he went on with his writing.

CHAPTER IV

After his first twenty-four hours in the hills the Professor was ready to swear that this final refuge was all he had hoped for. The situation (though he had hardly looked out on it) seemed high yet sheltered; he had a vague impression of sunshine in his room; and when he went down on the first morning, after a deep and curative sleep, he at once found himself in a congenial atmosphere. No effusive compatriots; no bowing and scraping French; only four or five English people, as much in dread of being spoken to as he was of their speaking to him. He consumed the necessary number of square inches of proteins and carbohydrates and withdrew to his room, as stubbornly ignored as if the other guests had all thought he was trying to catch their eyes. An hour later he was lost in his work.

If only life could ever remain on an even keel! But something had made him suspect it from the first: *there was a baby in the house*. Of course everybody denied it: the cook said the bowl of pap left by accident on the stairs was for the cat; the landlady said she had been a widow twenty years, and did he suppose--? And the *bonne* denied that there was a smell of paregoric on the landing, and said that was the way the scent of mimosa sometimes affected people.

That night, after a constitutional in the garden (ear-pads on), the Professor went up to his room to resume his writing. For

235

two hours he wrote uninterruptedly; then he was disturbed by a faint wail. He clapped on the pads, and continued; but the wail, low as it was, pierced them like a corkscrew. Finally he laid down his pen and listened, furiously. Every five minutes the sound came again. "I suppose they'll say it's a kitten!" he growled. No such pretence could deceive him for a moment; he remembered now that at the moment of entering the house he had noticed a smell of nursery. If only he had turned straight around and gone elsewhere! But where?

The idea of a fresh plunge into the unknown made him feel as weak as in the first stages of convalescence. And then his book had already sunk such talons into him; he could feel it sucking at his brain like some hungry animal. And all those people downstairs had been as cold and stony at dinner as they had at lunch. After two such encounters he was sure they would never bother him. A Paradise indeed, but for that serpent!

The wail continued, and he turned in his chair and looked slowly and desperately about him. The room was small and bare, and had only one door, the one leading into the passage. He vaguely recalled that, two nights before, at Monte Carlo, he had been disturbed in much the same way, and had found means to end the disturbance. What had he done? If only he could remember!

His eye went back to the door. There was a light under it

now; no doubt someone was up with the child. Slowly his mind dropped from the empyrean to the level of the crack under the door.

"A couple of towels...Ah, but, there are no towels!" Almost as the words formed themselves, his glance lit on a well-garnished rack. What had made him think there were no towels? Why, he had been reliving the night at Monte Carlo, where in fact, he now remembered, he could find none, and to protect himself from the noise next door had had to...

"Oh, my God!" shouted the Professor. His pen clattered to the floor. He jumped up, and his chair crashed after it. The baby, terror-struck, ceased to cry. There was an awful silence.

"Oh, my God!" shouted the Professor.

Slowly the vision of that other room came back: he saw himself jumping up just as wildly, dashing for towels and finding none, and then seizing a pile of papers and cramming them into the crack under the door. Papers, indeed! "Oh, my God..."

It was money that he had seized that other night: hundreds of hundred franc bills; or hundreds of thousands, were they? How furiously he had crushed and crumpled them in his haste to cram enough stuffing into the crack! Money--an unbelievable amount of it. But how in the world had it got there, to whom on earth did it belong?

The Professor sat down on the edge of the bed and took his

bursting head between his hands.

Daylight found him still labouring to reconstitute the succession of incredible episodes leading up to his mad act. Of all the piles of notes he had stuffed under the door not one franc had belonged to him. Of that he was now sure. He recalled also, but less clearly, that some one had given him a banknote--a hundred francs, he thought; was it on the steamer at Marseilles, or in the train?--given it with some mysterious injunction about gambling...that was as far as he could go at present...His mind had come down from the empyrean with a crash, and was still dazed from its abrupt contact with reality. At any rate, not a penny of the money was his, and he had left it all under the door in his hotel bedroom at Monte Carlo. And that was two days ago...

The baby was again crying, but the rest of the house still slept when, unkempt, unshorn, and with as many loose ends to his raiment as Hamlet, Professor Hibbart dashed out past an affrighted *bonne*, who cried after him that he might still catch the autobus if he took the short cut to the village.

To the Professor any abrupt emergence from his work was like coming to after a severe operation. He floated in a world as empty of ideas as of facts, and hemmed with slippery perpendicular walls. All the way to Monte Carlo those walls were made of the faces in the motorbus, blank inscrutable faces, smooth secret surfaces up which his mind struggled to clamber back to the actual. Only one definite

emotion survived: hatred of the being--a woman, was it?--
who had given him that fatal hundred franc note. He clung
to that feeling as to a life-belt, waiting doggedly till it should
lift him back to reality. If only he could have recalled his
enemy's name!

Arrived at Monte Carlo he hailed a taxi and pronounced
the one name he did recall: *Arcadie!* But what chance was
there that the first chauffeur he met would know the title, or
remember the site, of that undistinguished family hotel?

"*Arcadie?* But, of course! It's the place they're all asking for!"
cried the chauffeur, turning without a moment's hesitation
in what seemed to his fare to be the right direction. Yet how
could that obscure pension be the place "they" were all asking
for, and who in the name of madness were "they"?

"Are you sure--?" the Professor faltered.

"Of finding the way? *Allons donc*; we have only to follow
the crowd!"

This was a slight exaggeration, for at that early hour the
residential quarter of Monte Carlo was hardly more populous
than when the Professor had last seen it; but if he had doubted
being on the right road his doubt was presently dispelled by
the sight of a well-set-up young man in tennis flannels, with
a bright conversational eye, who came swinging along from
the opposite direction.

"Taber Tring!" cried a voice from the depths of the
Professor's sub-consciousness; and the Professor nearly flung

himself over the side of the taxi in the effort to attract his friend's notice.

Apparently he had been mistaken; for the young man, arrested by his signals, gave back a blank stare from eyes grown suddenly speechless, and then, turning on his heels, disappeared double-quick down a side-street. The Professor, thrown back into his habitual uncertainty, wavered over the question of pursuit; but the taxi was still moving forward, and before he could decide what to do it had worked its way through a throng of gaping people and drawn up before a gate surmounted by the well-remembered *Arcadie.*

"There you are!" the chauffeur gestured, with the air of a parent humouring a spoilt child.

There he was! The Professor started to jump out, and pushing through the crowd was confronted with a smoking ruin. The garden gate, under its lying inscription, led straight into chaos; and behind where *Arcadie* had stood, other houses, blank unknown houses, were also shouldering up to gape at the disaster.

"But this is not the place!" remonstrated the Professor. "This is a house that has burnt down!"

"*Parbleu,*" replied the chauffeur, still humouring him.

The Professor's temples were bursting.

"But was it--*was* it--was *this* the Hotel *Arcadie?*"

The chauffeur shrugged again and pointed to the name.

"When--did it burn?"

"Early yesterday."

"And the landlady--the person who kept it?"

"*Ah, ça...*"

"But how, in the name of pity, can I find out?"

The chauffeur seemed moved by his distress. "Let Monsieur reassure himself. There was no loss of life. If Monsieur had friends or relations..."

The Professor waved away the suggestion.

"We could, of course, address ourselves to the police," the chauffeur continued.

The police! The mere sound of the word filled his hearer with dismay. Explain to the police about that money? How could he--and in his French? He turned cold at the idea, and in his dread of seeing himself transported to the *commissariat* by the too-sympathetic driver, he hurriedly paid the latter off, and remained alone gazing through the gate at the drenched and smoking monument of his folly.

The money--try to get back the money? It had seemed almost hopeless before; now the attempt could only expose him to all the mysterious perils of an alien law. He saw himself interrogated, investigated, his passport seized, his manuscript confiscated, and every hope of rational repose and work annihilated for months to come. He felt himself curiously eyed by the policeman who was guarding the ruins, and turned from the scene of the disaster almost as hurriedly as the young man whom he had taken--no doubt

241

erroneously--for Taber Tring.

Having reached another quarter of the town, he sat down on a bench to take stock of his situation.

It was exactly what he had done two days before when, on arriving at Monte Carlo, he had found that he had missed the motorbus; and the associations of ideas once more came to his rescue.

Gradually there arose in his mind a faint wavering vision of a young woman, pearled and furred and scented, precipitately descending from his compartment, and, as she did so, cramming a banknote into his hand.

"The Princess...the Princess...*they call me Betsy at the dressmaker's...*" That was as far as the clue went; but presently the Professor remembered that his companion had got out of the train at Cannes, and it became certain to him that his only hope of clearing his overburdened conscience would be to take the train to that place, and there prosecute his almost hopeless search.

CHAPTER V

Not until he found himself seated in the train, and on the point of starting for Cannes, did the full horror of his situation break on the Professor. Then, for an hour, he contemplated it in all its intricate enormity, saw himself as a man dishonoured, ruined (for he now remembered the full amount of the sum he had to account for), and, worse still, severed from his best-loved work for a period incalculably long. For after he had struggled through the preliminary difficulties he would have to settle down to the slow task of reimbursement, and he knew that, to earn enough money to repay what he had lost, he must abandon serious scientific work such as he was now engaged in, and probably stoop--abominable thought!--to writing popular "science" articles in one of the illustrated magazines. Such a job had once been offered him on very handsome terms, and contemptuously rejected; and the best he could now hope was that there was still an opening for him somewhere between the Etiquette Column and the notes on Rachel powder and bathing tights.

Arrived at Cannes, he found his way to what appeared to be the fashionable shopping-street, and exteriorising his attention by an extreme effort of the will he began to go the rounds of the dressmaking establishments.

At every one he was received with distinguished politeness,

and every one, by some curious coincidence, had a Betsy to offer him. As the Betsies were all young, fluffy and rosy, considerable offence was caused by his rapid rejection of them, and it was in vain that he tried to close his ears to the crude and disobliging comments which on each occasion attended his retreat. But he had by this time regained a sufficiently clear vision of the Princess to be sure that she was not concealed behind any of the youthful substitutes proposed to him. In despair he issued from the last shop, and again sat himself down to consider.

As he did so, his mind gave a queer click, and the doors of his inner consciousness again swung open. But this time it was only to draw him back into the creative world from which he had been so violently ejected. He had suddenly seen a point to be made in the Einstein controversy, and he began to fumble for a paper on which to jot it down. He found only one, the closely-scribbled flap of a torn envelope on which, during the journey to Cannes, he had calculated and re-calculated the extent of the sum he would have to raise to reimburse the Princess; but possibly there might be a clear space on the other side. He turned it over, and there read, in a tall slanting hand:

Princesse Balalatinsky, *Villa Mon Caprice*, Route de Californie.

He started to his feet, and glanced about him frantically for a taxi. He had no idea where the Route de Californie was, but in his desperate circumstances, it seemed as easy to hire a taxi for a five minutes' transit as for a long expedition. Besides, it was the only way he knew of being sure of reaching his destination; and to do so as soon as possible was now a fixed idea.

The taxi carried him a long way; back through the whole length of the town, out on a flat white dusty road, and then up and up between walls overhung with luxuriant verdure till, at a turn, it stood still with a violent jerk.

The Professor looked out, and saw himself confronted by the expressive countenance of Mr. Taber Tring.

"Oh, my God--you again!" shrieked the young man, turning suddenly white with fury--or was it rather with fear?

"Why do you say *again?*" questioned the Professor; but his interlocutor, taking to his heels with unaccountable velocity, had already disappeared down a verdant by-way.

The Professor leaned back in the taxi in speechless amazement. He was sure now that the "again" referred to their previous encounter that morning at Monte Carlo, and he could only conclude that it had become a fixed habit of Taber Tring's to run away whenever they met, and that he ran a great deal too fast for the Professor ever to hope to overtake him.

"Well," said the driver, "there's a gentleman who isn't pleased. He thought I had no fare, and expected to get a lift up to the top of this mountain."

"I should have been happy to give him a lift," said the Professor rather wistfully; to which the driver replied: "He must be a mile off by this time. He didn't seem to fancy your looks."

There was no controverting this statement, mortifying as it was, and they continued their ascent till a gateway impressively crowned by heraldic lions admitted them to terraced gardens above which a villa of ample proportions looked forth upon the landscape.

The Professor was by this time so steeled to the unexpected that he hardly paused to consider the strange incongruity between the Princess's account of her fortunes and the setting in which she lived. He had read *Mon Caprice* on the gate, and that was the name on the envelope he had found in his pocket. With a resolute hand he rang the bell and asked a resplendent footman if the Princess Balalatinsky were at home.

He was shown through a long succession of drawing-rooms, in the last of which the Princess rose from the depths of a broad divan. She was dressed in black draperies, half-transparent--no, half-translucent; and she stood before the Professor in all the formidable completeness of her beauty.

Instantly his mind clicked again, and a voice shrilled up at him from the depths: "You always knew you could still recognize a beautiful woman when you saw one"; but he closed his ears to the suggestion and advanced toward the lady.

Before he could take more than three steps she was at his side, almost at his feet; her burning clasp was on his wrists, and her eyes were consuming him like coals of fire.

"Master! *Maestro!* Disguise is useless! You choose to come to me unannounced; but I was sure you would answer my appeal, and I should have recognized you anywhere, and among any number of people." She lifted his astonished hand to her lips. "It is the penalty of genius," she breathed.

"But--" gasped the Professor.

A scented finger was laid across his lips. "Hush: not yet. Let me tell you first why I ventured to write to you." She drew him gently down to an arm-chair beside the divan, and herself sank orientally into its pillows. "I thought I had exhausted all the emotions of life. At *my* age--is it not a tragedy? But I was mistaken. It is true that I had tried philosophy, marriage, mathematics, divorce, sculpture and love; but I had never attempted the stage. How long it sometimes takes to discover one's real vocation! No doubt you may have gone through the same uncertainties yourself. At any rate, my gift for the drama did not reveal itself till three months ago, and I have only just completed my play, The Scarlet Cataract,' a picture of my life, as the title suggests--and which, my friends tell me, is not without dramatic merit. In fact, if I were to listen to them..."

The Professor struggled from his seat. His old fear of her madness had returned. He began very mildly: "It is quite natural that you should mistake me for some one else--"

With an inimitable gesture she waved the interruption aside. "But what I want to explain is that, of course, the leading role can have but one interpreter--Myself. The things happened to *Me*: who else could possibly know how to act them? Therefore, if I appeal to you--on my knees, Illustrious Impresario!--it is in my double character as dramatist and tragédienne; for in spite of appearances my life *has* been a tragedy, as you will acknowledge if you will let me outline its principal events in a few words..."

But here she had to pause a second for breath, and the Professor, on his feet, actually shouted his protest. "Madam, I cannot let you go on another moment, first because I've heard the story of your life already, and secondly because I'm not the man you suppose."

The Princess turned deadly pale. "Impostor!" she hissed, and reached for an embroidered bell-rope.

Her agitation had the curious effect of calming the Professor. "You had better not send me away," he said, "till you learn why I am here. I am the unhappy man to whom, the day before yesterday, you entrusted a hundred franc note which you asked him to stake for you at Monte Carlo. Unfortunately I could not recall your name or address, and I have been hunting for you through all the dressmakers' establishments in Cannes."

The instant lighting-up of her face was a sight so lovely that he almost forgot his apprehensions and his shame.

"The dressmakers' shops? Ah--in search of 'Betsy'! It is true, I was obliged to act as a *mannequin* for one day; but since then my fortunes have miraculously changed--changed thanks to you; for now," the Princess continued with enthusiasm, "I do at last recognise my good angel, my benefactor of the other day, and ask myself how I could have failed to know you again, how I could have taken you for a vulgar theatrical manager, you, a man of genius and a Philosopher. Can you ever forgive me? For I owe you everything--everything--everything!" she sobbed out, again almost at his knees.

His self-possession continued to increase in proportion to her agitation. He actually risked laying a hand on her arm and pressing her mildly back among her cushions.

"Only a change of pronouns," he said sighing, "is necessary to the complete accuracy of your last statement."

But she was off again on a new tack. "That blessed hundred franc note! From the moment when you took it from me, as I got out of the train, my luck miraculously and completely changed. I knew you were going to win some money for me; but how could I have imagined the extent of the fortune you were to heap at my feet?"

A cold sweat broke out over the Professor. She knew, then--once again her infernal intuition had pierced his secret! In the train had she not discovered his name, identified him as the author of "The Elimination of Phenomena," and guessed that he was actually engaged in the composition of another work? At the moment he had fancied that there was a plausible explanation for each of these discoveries; but he now felt that her powers of divination were in need of no outward aid. She had risen from her seat and was once more in possession of his hands.

"You have come to be thanked--and I do thank you!" Her heavy lashes glittered with tears which threatened to merge with the drops of moisture rolling down the Professor's agonized brow.

"Don't--don't, I beg!" He freed himself and shrank back. "If you'll only let me speak...let me explain..."

She raised a reproachful finger. "Let you belittle yourself? Let you reject my gratitude? No--no! Nothing that you can say can make any difference. The gipsy in the Caucasus told me long ago what you were going to do for me. And now that you have done it you want to stifle the thanks on my lips!"

"But you have nothing to thank me for. I have made no money for you--on the contrary, I--"

"Hush, hush! Such words are blasphemy. Look about you at all this luxury, this beauty. I expected to have to leave it tomorrow. And thanks to you, wealth has poured in on me at the moment when I thought I was face to face with ruin."

"Madam, you must let me undeceive you. I don't know who can have brought you such an erroneous report." The Professor glanced about him in acute distress, seeking to escape from her devouring scrutiny. "It is true that I did make a considerable sum for you, but I--I afterward lost it. To my shame be it said."

The Princess hardly appeared to hear him. Tears of gratitude still rained down her face. "Lost it? A little more, a little less--what does it matter? In my present pecuniary situation nothing of that sort counts. I am rich--rich for life! I should, in fact," she continued with a gush of candour, "be an absolutely happy woman if I could only find an impresario who would stage my play." She lifted her enchanting eyes to his. "I wonder, by the way, dear friend," she proposed, "if you would let me read it to you now?"

"Oh, no, no," the Professor protested; and then, becoming aware of the offence his words were likely to give, he added precipitately: "Before we turn to any other subject you must really let me tell you just how much money I owe you, and what were the unfortunate circumstances in which..."

But he was conscious that the Princess was no longer listening to him. A new light had dawned in her face, and the glow of it was already drying her tears. Slim, palpitating and girlish, she turned toward one of the tall French windows opening upon the terrace.

"My fiance--your young compatriot! Here he is! Oh, how happy I am to bring you together!" she exclaimed.

The Professor followed her glance with a stare of fresh amazement. Through the half-open window a young man in tennis flannels had strolled into the room.

"My Taber," the Princess breathed, "this is my benefactor- -*our* benefactor--this is..."

Taber Tring gently removed the perfect arms which were already tightening about his neck. "I know who he is," he said in a hard high tone. "That's why I've been running away from him ever since early this morning."

His good-humoured boyish face was absolutely decomposed by distress. Without vouchsafing the least attention to the Princess he stood pallidly but resolutely facing her visitor.

"I've been running for all I was worth; at least till a quarter of an hour ago. Then I suddenly pulled up short and said to myself: 'Taber Tring, this won't do. You were born in the Middle West, but your parents came from New England, and now's the time to prove it if you're ever going to. Stern and rockbound coast, and *Mayflower* and all the rest of it. If there's anything in it, it ought to come out now.' And, by George it *did*; and here I am, ready to make a clean breast of it."

He drew a silk handkerchief from his pocket, and wiped his brow, which was as damp with agony as the Professor's. But the Professor's patience had reached its final limit, and he was determined, whatever happened, to hold all interrupters at bay till he had made a clean breast of his own.

"I don't know, sir," he said, "why you avoided my presence this morning nor why you now seek it; but since you are connected with this lady by so close a tie, there is no reason why I should not continue in your presence what I had begun to tell her. I repeat then, Madam, that with your hundred franc note in my hand, I approached a table and staked the sum with results so unexpectedly and incredibly favourable that I left the gaming-rooms just before midnight in possession of--"

"Ninety-nine thousand seven hundred francs and no centimes," Taber Tring interposed.

The Professor received this with a gasp of astonishment; but everything which was happening was so foreign to all the laws of probability as experienced at Purewater that it did not long arrest his attention.

"You have stated the sum accurately," he said; "but you do not know that I am no longer in possession of a penny of it."

"Oh, don't I?" groaned Taber Tring, wiping a fresh outbreak of moisture from his forehead.

The Professor stopped short. "You do know? Ah, but to be sure. You were yourself a fellow-boarder at *Arcadie*. You were perhaps under its roof when that disastrous fire broke out and destroyed the whole of the large sum of money I had so negligently left--"

"Under the door!" shrieked Taber Tring. "Under the door of your room, which happened to be the one next to mine."

A light began to dawn on the Professor. "Is it possible that you were the neighbour whose unseasonable agitation during the small hours of the night caused me, in the total absence of towels or other available material, to stuff the money in question under the crack of the door in order to continue my intellectual labours undisturbed?"

"That's me," said Taber Tring sullenly.

But the Princess, who had been listening to the Professor's disquisition with a look of lovely bewilderment gradually verging on boredom, here intervened with a sudden flash of attention.

"What sort of noises proceeded from my Taber's room at that advanced hour of the night?" she inquisitorially demanded of the Professor.

"Oh, shucks," said her betrothed in a weary tone. "Aren't they all alike, every one of 'em?" He turned to the Professor. "I daresay I *was* making a noise. I was about desperate. Stony broke, and didn't know which way to turn next. I guess *you'd* have made a noise in my place."

The Professor felt a stirring of sympathy for the stricken youth. "I'm sorry for you--very sorry," he said. "If I had known your situation I should have tried to master my impatience, and should probably not have crammed the money under the door; in which case it would not have been destroyed in the fire..."

("How like the reflexions of a Chinese sage!" the Princess admiringly murmured.)

"Destroyed in the fire? It wasn't," said Taber Tring.

The Professor reeled back and was obliged to support himself upon the nearest chair. "It wasn't?"

"Trust me," said the young man. "I was there, and I stole it."

"You stole it--his money?" The Princess instantly flung herself on his bosom. "To save your beloved from ruin? Oh, how Christlike--how Dostoyevskian!" She addressed herself with streaming eyes to the Professor. "Oh, spare him, sir, for heaven's sake spare him! What shall I do to avert your vengeance? Shall I prostitute myself in the streets of Cannes? I will do anything to atone to you for his heroic gesture in stealing your money--"

Taber Tring again put her gently aside. "Do drop it, Betsy. This is not a woman's job. I stole that money in order to gamble with it, and I've got to pay it back, and all that I won with it too." He paused and faced about on the Professor. "Isn't that so, sir?" he questioned. "I've been puzzling over it day and night for the last two days, and I can't figure it out any other way. Hard on you, Betsy, just as we thought our fortune was made; but my firm conviction, Professor Hibbart, as a man of New England stock, is that at this moment I owe you the sum of one million seven hundred and fifty thousand francs."

"My God," screamed the Professor, "what system did you play?"

Mr. Tring's open countenance snapped shut like a steel trap. "That's my secret," he said politely; and the Professor had to acknowledge that it was.

"I must ask you," the young man pursued, "to be good enough either to disprove or to confirm my estimate of my indebtedness to you. How much should you consider that you owed if you had stolen anybody's money and made a lot more with it? Only the sum stolen or the whole amount? There's my point."

"But I did! I have!" cried the Professor. "Did what?"

"Exactly what you have done. Stole--that is, gambled with a sum of money entrusted to me for the purpose, and won the large amount you have correctly stated. It is true," the Professor continued, "that I had no intention of appropriating a penny of it; but, believing that my culpable negligence had caused the whole sum to be destroyed by fire, I considered myself--"

"Well?" panted Taber Tring.

"As indebted for the entire amount to this lady here--"

Taber Tring's face became illuminated with sudden comprehension.

"Holy Moses I You don't mean to say all that money under

the door belonged to Betsy?"

"Every cent of it, in my opinion," said the Professor firmly; and the two men stood and stared at each other.

"But, good gracious," the Princess intervened, "then nobody has stolen anything!"

The load which had crushed the Professor to earth rolled from his shoulders, and he lifted the head of a free man. "So it would seem."

But Taber Tring could only ejaculate once again: "Holy Moses!"

"Then we are rich once more--is it not so, my Taber?" The Princess leaned a thoughtful head upon her hand. "Do you know, I could almost regret it? Yes, I regret, dear friends, that you are both blameless, and that no sacrifice will be demanded of me. It would have been so beautiful if you had both sinned, and I had also had to sin to save you. But, on the other hand," she reflected, with lifted eyes and a smile like heaven, "I shall now be able to have my play brought out at my own expense. And for that," she cried, again possessing herself of Professor Hibbart's hands, "for that too I have to thank you! And this is the only way I know of doing it."

She flung her arms around his neck and lifted her lips to his; and the exonerated and emancipated Professor took what she offered like a man.

"And now," she cried, "for my other hero!" and caught her betrothed to her heart. These effusions were interrupted by the entrance of the resplendent footman, who surveyed them without surprise or disapproval.

"There is at the door," he announced, "a young lady of the name of Betsy who is asking for Monsieur." He indicated the Professor. "She would give no other name; she said that was enough. She knows Monsieur has been seeking her everywhere in Cannes, and she is in despair at having missed him; but at the time she was engaged with another client."

The Professor turned pale, and Taber Tring's left lid sketched a tentative wink.

But the Princess intervened in her most princely manner. "Of course! My name is Betsy, and you were seeking for *me* at all the dressmakers'!" She turned to the footman with her smile of benediction. "Tell the young lady," she said, "that Monsieur in his turn is engaged with another client, who begs her to accept this slight compensation for her trouble." She slipped from her wrist a hoop of jade and brilliants, and the footman withdrew with the token.

"And now," said the Princess, "as it is past three o'clock, we ought really to be thinking of *zakouska*."